Rose Zwi was born in Oaxaco, Mexico, in 1928, and has lived in South Africa most of her life. In 1967, she graduated as a mature student in English Literature from the University of the Witwatersrand. She worked for some years as an editor at Ravan Press, Johannesburg, a small publisher that concentrated mainly on black writing. She was also active in Black Sash, a women's civil rights organisation, for many years. Her first novel, *Another Year in Africa,* won the Olive Schreiner Prize. In 1988 she left South Africa, just one year before the release of political prisoners and the beginning of the 'new' South Africa. She now lives in New South Wales, and is married with three adult children.

Other books by Rose Zwi:

Another Year in Africa
The Inverted Pyramid
Exiles
The Umbrella Tree

SAFE HOUSES

Rose Zwi

SPINIFEX

Spinifex Press Pty Ltd
504 Queensberry Street
North Melbourne, Vic. 3051
Australia

First published by Spinifex Press, 1993

Typeset by Nicole Prowse, Melbourne
Printed in Australia by Australian Print Group
Cover design by Lin Tobias

National Library of Australia
Cataloguing-in-Publication entry:

Zwi, Rose.
    Safe Houses.

    ISBN 1 875559 21 3.

    I. Title.

A823.3

ONE

I, Zalman Shenker, was born three days before Pesach, on the night Janka Shtaba's barn burned down, in the year 1903.

What more need I say? I was born, I am living, I shall die. Write, you urge me, write! What for? Who for? For me, you answer, for my children. Unless we know about the past ... I smile. Who learns from the past? But what else is there to write about? The present? That's why I'm writing, to use it up. The future? Too grim. And the present is the no-man's land between them.

Also, dear niece, I suspect your motives. You're trying to keep me occupied, out of mischief. You have the soul of a social worker, no sense of the innate tragedy of life. For you everything must have meaning, every problem a solution. At forty-nine, married, mother of grown children, you're still trying to change the world. Dare I tell you a secret? I hesitate ... Lola, this all-too-solid world does not exist. We are living in a nightmare dreamed by god, who is so locked into it that he cannot wake, and we, poor creatures, have to act out his sick fantasies. No. I dare not tell you. You will put on your black

1

sash and protest so loudly that either god will wake – and where will that leave us? – or you'll have me moved from the Aged Home to the Insane Home. The young (forty-nine is young from where I am) play god with us too.

Aged Home, Insane Home, this home, that home. I looked up the word in the dictionary the other day because I no longer know what it means. A dwelling place, they call it; a fixed residence of a family or a household. With a capital H, it is an institution of refuge or rest for persons needing care. And the long or last home means the grave. From birth to death, then, man is always in a home. Woman also, I hasten to add. My dear Lola, I do not dislike or disrespect women. On the contrary, my esteem for Woman is so great, that I never inflicted marriage on Her.

A house, on the other hand, is not a home. A famous Madam once made that distinction. The dictionary says a house is a building for human habitation. I, therefore, live in a Home; this cannot be described as a place for human habitation. My emphasis is on human; I have nothing against the structure itself, blatantly institutional though it is. But cast your eye over us decrepit inhabitants and you'll see what I mean.

Yes, Lola, I've succumbed. I'm going to write in this black-covered notebook. By the time I have filled it, it will be black inside as well. I shall will it to you; what else can I leave you besides a few tattered books? But you will get it only after I am dead. And then you will struggle with it. Your Yiddish is of the kitchen variety and I rather pride myself on my style. This way I can write freely without upsetting or angering anyone. As though that ever held you back, I hear my family sneer, mostly from the grave. They should only know how much I left unsaid.

Let me show you my world, Lola, as I see it. On this side of the valley are the Homes; on the other side, the houses. The Homes are where the discards of society are shunted for safe keeping: the ex-soldiers, the insane, the old, the crippled, the diseased. In the houses live people still embroiled with Life, which, however, is driving them inexorably towards the Homes. The deluded creatures believe they'll be young forever. I'll

2

rephrase what a black rebel once said to a white man who was praising the matchbox houses of Soweto: I'm pleased you like the Aged Home; you'll be living here yourself one day.

The houses begin at the brow of the hills that run from east to west, and flow into the suburbs below, where they lie in cool green gardens with swimming pools and tennis courts. Separating the houses from the Homes is a golf course – when I say gulf course you think I'm mispronouncing it – that slopes gently into the valley through which a sluggish river trickles, dividing the two worlds as though it was as wide and as deep as the Volga. On the upward slope, towards the Homes, is a suburb of houses built in the late forties for soldiers who fought in the Second World War, the Just War. I sometimes wonder if they still live there. I often see young women wheeling prams in the area. Perhaps they don't know about the old soldiers. Perhaps they don't even know about the War. The young are not concerned with history, with origins. They think they're inventing everything anew. But I digress. Let me return to my origins.

As I said, I was born three days before Pesach, on the night Janka Shtaba's barn burned down. That's how dates were calculated in our shtetl; in relation to the holy days and to memorable events. It mattered little what date the clerk scribbled down on the birth or death certificates: we remembered our way. Like John Sibiya, a black man who has worked at the Home for over thirty years. He lives in the township a few kilometres north of our Home, and he walks to work every day, in rain, frost or heat. He tells me he was born two years after the 'Flu Epidemic, and two years before the miners' big strike. That makes it about 1920, which means he is seventeen years younger than I am. I'd have sworn he was older. I can't tell age in black people.

By all accounts, I was a good-looking child. I've got photographs of myself from the age of sixteen which bear this out. (You'll find the photographs in my grey suitcase, under my bed.) I was tall and slim, with large brown eyes under arched eyebrows that even then regarded the world with the contempt it deserves. My nose was straight and thin, and my mouth, the feature I liked least, was full and curved, like a girl's. It flattened out and looked more masculine after I had my teeth out and was fitted with dentures. But that was many years later.

And by all accounts, I was brilliant. I think I remembered everything I ever read. Which cluttered up my mind with so much information, that it did not leave space for real understanding. For example, I still remember, word-perfect and in Hebrew, how god discomfitted all Joshua's enemies and slew them with a great slaughter at Gibeon, and chased them along the way that goeth up to Beth-horon, and smote them to Azekah, and unto Makkedah. And how the sun stood still in the midst of heaven and hastened not to go down for a whole day. And there was no day like that before it or after it. And all because Joshua required it.

I wish I were on such good terms with god. I would ask him for short days and even shorter nights. I'm getting weary of this life. And even more weary of writing about it. This writing is a bad idea; it makes me more irritable than ever. I shall not write.

I'll smile, Lola, when you ask how it's getting on, and say nothing. I'll outwit you yet. Practise your social work on others.

TWO

As Lola walks into the vestibule, she looks up at the tapestry on the south wall. At its centre is a brown-skinned Christ-figure with long black hair, a moustache and a beard. He is wearing an African caftan and has a coppery halo around his head. Stitched across the top of the tapestry is the word for peace, in six languages: KAGISO, UXOLO, KHOTSO, PEACE, UKUTHULA, VREDE. He could be a mixture of any of the people speaking these languages: Tswana, Xhosa, Sotho, English, Zulu and Afrikaans. Images of rural African life, with a church, are sewn in bright colours on his right. Urban life, with a larger church, is represented on his left by tall buildings, a headgear and mine dumps. People, in various shades of brown, mill about him, and to the side of the buildings stands a woman of greenish-grey complexion, with a black sash tied diagonally from shoulder to waist. She is holding a placard: ABOLISH PASS LAWS.

Listen to the lady, Lola appeals to the Christ-figure; abolish the pass laws. He does not even glance at the placard. Nor does He see the queue which straggles out of the waiting room on the mezzanine floor, down the stairs, and into the vestibule. He gazes sadly through the glass doors onto the street, where other black people are hurrying to work from the Noord Street bus terminus.

Why, Lola wonders as she walks towards the stone stairs, do I always think of Him with a capital H? I'm not even an observant Jew, let alone a Christian. I'm becoming like Uncle Zalman, an unrelenting agnostic who is constantly invoking God. "When people don't listen," Zalman tells her, "you talk to god. Not that he listens, but that doesn't matter, since we don't know if he exists." Zalman doesn't think of any deity in capital letters. She loves Zalman, difficult and obstinate though he is. She hopes he will become so involved in writing his memoirs, that he stops subverting the discipline at the Home. An octagenarian rebel can be more disruptive than a twenty-year-old rebel. She should know. She is closely related to both.

Lola is not sure to whom ABOLISH PASS LAWS is addressed – to Jesus or to the Government. Neither is responding. If only they would. The Advice Office might then close down, and her labours in the salt mines would cease. Some hope. Even if the pass laws were abolished, the poverty would remain, together with the injustice and the oppression. The salt mines, she concludes, are created by human tears, and to these there is no end.

This building once belonged to the Automobile Association. Now it is home to church groups, trade unions and other opponents of apartheid. It is square, the four sides forming a well in the centre. The vestibule has a domed roof and the light that streams down the well through the spherical skylights embedded in the dome, illuminates the tapestry. On each side of the tapestry are two double doors, one leading to a hall, the other to a small chapel where daily services are held for the workers in the building. In its AA days, clerks and officials had stood behind a semi-circular counter on the ground floor, dispensing maps and information about travel, issuing international drivers' licences, and giving advice about the best routes to pleasure resorts throughout the country. Staff and clients, then, had been mostly white. Today the building could be standing in the heart of Africa.

The stone stairs up which Lola is walking lead to a mezzanine floor, between the ground and first floors. The other six floors are reached by a lift on the far side of the vestibule. Security is lax. One bomb blast ... Lola shudders. There have been a few arson attempts. We'll investigate, the police always say, and that is where the matter ends. Complaining to the cause about the effect. She looks through the open doors of the hall; the chairs are still in disarray after last night's meeting. From the chapel, on the other side of the tapestry, come the sweet strains of a hymn; the morning service is in progress. Not only have they got rhythm, she parodies the old racist cliché; they also sing so well. She hopes God appreciates the music, even if the words are sometimes subverted for the Cause, known these days as the Struggle.

There she goes again: God, God, God.

She moves slowly through the crowd, greeting people as she edges her way up. She pauses to catch breath: she must lose weight and start exercising. The steps are already littered with cigarette butts, sweet papers and orange peel. A smell of coal fires, burned in crowded rooms, wafts off coats, shawls and sweaters. How different they are from the perfumed clientele of the Automobile Association: mothers humped by their babies, men in livery, their employers' names branded on chest and back; old men leaning on walking sticks, and old women, feet ballooning over misshapen shoes, carrying family histories in plastic shopping bags: birth certificates, death notices, rent receipts and hire-purchase agreements. By the time they reach the counsellors, they will be dry-mouthed and exhausted. Some will be helped, a few may be comforted. The rest will have to wait for a more equitable dispensation. Yet they keep coming, if only to be heard. People are still listening, Uncle Zalman, but I don't know if God is. All the desks in the first office are occupied. Mary and Dorothy, veterans of the organisation, work with three black women who are training to open advice offices in the townships. They make notes, photocopy specimen affidavits and, as none of the white counsellors speaks a Bantu language, act as interpreters. The room is crowded, and everyone seems to be talking at once, in varying degrees of loudness, in at least three languages.

"Good of you to come," Mary extends her usual welcome to Lola.

Mary, a tall, striking woman in her sixties, has been working in the office for over twenty years. If she sounds like a gracious hostess welcoming a guest to a tea party, albeit to a Mad Hatter's tea party, it is because Lola is still regarded as a relative newcomer, whose commitment to the work is shaky.

"How does one face the victims of one's privileged life?" she once asked Mary, "when so little can be done for them?" "You do what you can," Mary had replied briskly.

Lola regrets having left her job at Marriage Guidance. "Giving advice about marriage," Paul used to scoff. "Have you no humility?" "Other people's problems are easier to solve," she had replied. But it was Michael who had finally goaded her into leaving. "If you're concerned about broken families, Ma, go and work at the Advice Office. Migrant workers and township blacks need help more than your suburban sisters. I'll get you a T-shirt: DON'T DO GOOD; DO BETTER."

She feels inadequate and frustrated at the Advice Office, but is ashamed to leave after such a short time. She has, however, thought of a compromise: As there is no time to do the correspondence during office hours, Mary and Dorothy reply to letters at night and over weekends. If she offers to do it, their workload will be lightened and she will not have to sit in the office and watch hope drain from people's faces as she says, "Sorry, sorry, sorry … the laws, you know … nothing we can do." "Nothing?" they echo with despair. "Nothing, Medem? Hau, and what must I do now? And where must I get the help?"

This will also give her time to consult with the experienced counsellors. The little she knows, she has learned from Mary. She listens as Mary informs people of their rights, explains unemployment benefits, directs a widow to the Pensions Office, or confronts an employer who has dismissed a worker without leave pay or notice pay. Mary is especially knowledgeable about Section 10 rights – the main bulwark against the dreaded pass laws which are designed to keep black people out of the urban areas.

Lola has not yet mastered the intricacies of this complicated Act from which one has to squeeze all possible concessions. A mistake could cost a person his or her right to live and work in town. When in doubt, Mary has told her, ask either Dorothy or me.

Dorothy looks over her spectacles and greets Lola warmly. She is a large, attractive woman in her late forties who, in addition to being the Director of the Advice Office, also works for other human rights groups. The daughter of one of the founders of the organisation, she cut her teeth on the pass laws, took her first steps with migrant labour, and knows more about mass removals, land acts, tribal customs and industrial relations than most lawyers, anthropologists, or trade unionists. Dorothy and Mary, both practising Christians, draw strength from their faith, Lola guesses. But what sustains Edna, she wonders as she sits down at an empty desk in the office next door. Edna is a vivacious, non-observant Jewish woman in her late fifties, who is supervising two young German voluntary workers. "Expiating the sins of their fathers," she has said to Lola, "but who isn't? Still, I'd rather be training black people to help themselves. Just as these girl guides of the western world learn to distinguish between Section 10 (1) (a) and Section 10 (1) (b), they flit off to another country, to do-good there."

"Hello, Lola. Good you're here," Edna says. "Did you see the queue? We've got a helluva day ahead. Before I forget. We're organising a protest for the fourteenth. Remind me to give you the details."

Lola smiles, but says nothing. Standing on street corners with placards reading, TROOPS OUT OF THE TOWNSHIPS or CHARGE OR RELEASE, is ineffectual; you convince nobody. Those who agree with you, wave or give a thumbs-up as they drive past; the others hang out of car windows, bang on their doors, and shout out obscenities. Even Jesus ignores the grey-green woman on the tapestry whose placard appeals for the abolition of the pass laws.

Political faith; that's what keeps Edna going. And because Lola herself is not a believer, religious or political, she cannot dedicate herself to this heartbreaking work. She sighs, relieved to find a reason – or an excuse – for her lack of commitment.

Even as a teenager, after World War II, when millenarian dreams had swept through a shell-shocked world, she had distanced herself from such utopianism. She had grown up in an apolitical home. Her father, a property developer, had worked a ten-hour day; her mother, a dynamic charity worker, had organised bridge drives, morning markets and lavish luncheons in their manorial home. "Not," Uncle Zalman used to say, "because Baila feels pity for the orphaned, the poor or the handicapped, but because she needs to wipe out the memory of a deprived childhood in the shtetl."

Zalman, as usual, had exaggerated; he had always had a horror of 'good works'. But Lola had never questioned her mother's values; she had been a compliant daughter. An only child, she had known from an early age what was expected of her: a pre-matrimonial BA, marriage to a doctor or a lawyer, and later, when her children were older, voluntary work for the African Children's Feeding scheme, the SPCA or some other organisation.

Tall, attractive, with dark curly hair and deep blue eyes under winged brows, Lola might have fulfilled her mother's expectations had she not met Paul, a wild-haired anthropology tutor, with high cheek bones and moody green eyes; a failed idealist, she was told, who was on the rebound from a broken love affair. Heathcliff: she wondered who his Cathy was. She enrolled for his course. "How did a bourgeois popke like you stray into Social Anthropology?" he had asked. "You should be doing Bibstuds, History of Art or Italian Special." "I am," she had replied. "And I'm majoring in French." Disconcerted by her candour and by her refusal to conceal her unworthy bourgeois aspirations, he decided to take her in hand. The first time they made love she discovered who his Cathy was; "Ruth," he sighed as he rolled over. But she loved him so much, she was certain she would drive other loves from his heart. Many years later, at

Marriage Guidance, she encountered other sufferers from this delusionary syndrome.

Like Zalman says when he is reprimanded by the Director of the Home for his misdeeds: anyone can make a mistake.

As Lola adjusts the carbon paper in her Day Book in which each interview is recorded, she listens to Lina, one of the German women, direct her petitioner to the Industrial Aid Society. Client, customer, supplicant, solicitor, patient; Lola never knows what to call these distressed people. Anything but Cases, Mary has told her sternly. Lola envies Lina's detachment, her confidence. It seems to come so naturally to these young people. In no time at all they have been to all the black townships, squatter camps and resettlement areas; met up with student leaders and trade unionists; protested, demonstrated and mourned at mass funerals, and sung 'Inkosi Sikelel' iAfrika' at meetings without a trace of self-consciousness, elbows angled, fists clenched. Lola doesn't even know the words of 'God Save the Queen'.

Students, church groups, civil-rights workers and other visitors from abroad, stream into the office. Here, they say, one gets a picture of what is really happening in the country. Lola is surprised; she does not know what is really happening in the country.

"Have you been here before?" she asks the young man whom Sophie, one of the black translators, has brought to her desk. He has edged his way around the other people in the crowded office and sits down on a stool, bestowing a trusting smile on her. "May I see your reference book," she says when he tells her this is his first visit, "your pass?"

"My reverence book!" He leaps up and feels for it in his back pocket. She has often seen this jittery reaction. Pass, kaffir! the police shout, demanding identification and speeding up the process with a punch to the head or a kick in the groin.

She takes the plastic-covered reference book, warm and rounded by the shape and temperature of his haunches – such an intimate act, probing a person's identity – and opens it to the back page. There is a photograph of the man, his name, identity number, race group – Tswana in this case – and the year of his birth. She enters this information in the Day Book then says, "What is your problem, Mr Mpete?" "My problem is," the man says, and her day in the office begins.

Lola's cases – how else can she refer to them? – are relatively straightforward until a dignified woman of about forty, wearing a neat cotton dress and a scarf tied low over her forehead, sits down at the desk.

"Hello, Medem," she says, putting down her shopping bag. "I need the help for a beth stiffcat."

"A beth stiffcat?" Lola repeats loudly, catching Edna's eye.

"Draw up an affidavit," Edna tells her, "applying for a birth certificate."

"I must get the poymit to live in Soweto," the woman explains, recognising a novice, "so I must first have the beth stiffcat."

"Of course," Lola says, "you need a birth certificate before they will give you a permit to live in Soweto."

The woman nods approvingly; Lola is a fast learner.

By one o'clock she has seen nine people. Except for a half-hour break in the little room between the advisors' offices and the general office where the typists and the telephonist work, counselling continues until there is no one left in the queue. As Lola bites into her sandwich, she hears the hum of conversation from the waiting room, and smells the vinegared potato chips, oranges and cigarette smoke. Counsellors and counselled at their separate lunches.

"The police seem to wait for the coldest night of the year to demolish shacks," Dorothy is saying, as she pours herself a cup of tea. "The squatters have no place to go. People from the townships are taking them in. I've spoken to the lawyers and to the press. Twenty people were injured when the bull-dozers moved in."

"Trouble again with security firms," Edna says, peeling an orange. "Five guards were dismissed without notice or leave pay because they'd asked for overtime pay. The worst kind of ruffians are running these security companies, mostly ex-policemen. They beat their workers and starve the guard dogs, but the demand for private home security is so great these days that they're sprouting like dragons' teeth all over the country. The manager refused to talk to me when I phoned him. Blerry communist, he called me. I sent the dismissed men to the Department of Manpower. Fat lot of good that'll do. I wish the trade unions would get moving."

"It's happening," Dorothy assures her, gesturing towards the offices on the other side of the passage where the Caterers' Union has recently moved in.

After the lunch break, Sophie ushers in a thin young boy wearing a short-sleeved shirt, torn trousers and dirty tackies without socks. He shivers, averts his eyes from Lola's and wipes his nose with the back of his hand. He stares down at his shoes as Sophie slowly extracts his story from him.

"He was born in his grandmother's house in Alexandra township," Sophie translates from the boy's halting Zulu. "He cannot read or write in any language. His mother died when he was born and he never knew his father ... When he was about two years old, his grandmother died and he was sent to a relative in a small village in kwaZulu where he herded cattle until this man also died ... His widow beat him so much that he ran away and tried to find his way back to his family but he couldn't remember the address ... The houses, they all look the same. All he knows is that his name is Lucky Nkosi and that his grandmother's name was Betty Nkosi.

"Nkosi," Sophie adds, "is like Smith or Cohen. Too many people are called Nkosi. And he doesn't even know his mother's name," she says, blowing her nose loudly into a crumpled strip of toilet paper. The black translators try to distance themselves from the troubles of the supplicants; they have enough of their own in the townships.

He's about sixteen, Lola thinks; four years younger than Michael and half his size.

"He lived in the veld," Sophie continues, "doing jobs for food. Now he is cleaning for a shebeen queen ... The police always drink at the shebeen and he must hide, because he hasn't

13

got a reference book and he hasn't got money to bribe them …
His grandmother did not register his birth, so he cannot get a
reference book. What must he do?"

Not only is there no evidence that he was born in Johannesburg; there is no proof that he exists at all. As Edna is busy
with a group of squatters, Lola takes him through to Mary.

"We must draw up affidavits as truthfully as we can," Mary
tells her, "in order to establish an identity for the child. Many
children are sent into the rural areas to be raised by relatives, so
we have no reason to doubt his word. Sophie, tell him to bring
in the reference books of two people, preferably women, who
remember his birth. You are a naive dimwit, Lola: I know he
can't trace his family, but someone must have been present at
his birth, and if we can't find the exact people, surrogate
witnesses will have to do. I mean, he was born, wasn't he? Here
he is, living proof of that fact. We shall have to make up, I mean
type, one affidavit in his name, giving his life history, and two
supporting affidavits from the putative birth witnesses. I don't
know if it'll work, but we'll try. Sophie, tell him to see me when
he comes in again with the documents. Lola, open a file giving
all the information we have about him."

Why, Lola wonders as she takes a yellow folder from Mary's
desk, does anyone bother to write fiction when reality pre-empts anything one can invent? Only in affidavits should one
write fiction.

At the end of the day, Lola goes in to Mary's office. She will
offer to do the correspondence; she cannot bear to work here.
Mary is speaking to a shabbily dressed man with grey pepper-corn hair.

"I'm sorry," she is saying. "Our organisation has no funds.
But I've written a letter to the social worker in your area asking
her to help you while we try to get your South African citizen-ship reinstated. Then you will be able to get a pension."

She hands him the letter, together with five rand which she
takes out of her purse. "For bus fare," she says to him. Her eyes
are blazing as she pulls on her overcoat.

"We'll fry in hell for all this misery," she says, "for eternity."

Lola postpones her request to do the correspondence. She walks out of the office with Mary whom she would like to know better. Perhaps she will ask her to dinner one evening. Everyone has left except the cleaner who is stacking the chairs and sweeping the floor. The vestibule is empty, but Lola still hears the shuffling feet, the muted sighs, the cry of babies, the drift of hymns from the chapel.

A cold blast of air hits them as they step outside. Muffled-up people are streaming towards the railway station or the bus terminus. It is only five-thirty but the sun is sinking rapidly behind the buildings at the end of the street. By the time the black commuters reach their townships, they will have to walk through unlit, smoky streets, in total darkness.

Mary folds her tall, gaunt body into her battered Volkswagen, and rolling down her window says, "You and your husband must come for dinner one evening. Next Friday? I'm having a charming couple over whom I'm sure you'd like. Ruth Singer and her husband Daniel. She worked at the office for a while, but is now writing, full time."

Lola's stomach knots up. Again Ruth has been there before her.

"Thanks, we'd love to come but can we make it some other time? Paul will be out of town next week."

"Some other time then," Mary says, grinding into gear. "I look forward to meeting Paul. I believe he's doing wonderful work as an anthropologist on the mines."

Lola watches Mary's car slip into the north-bound traffic that will take her to the ex-servicemen's suburb where she lives, just a stone's throw from Uncle Zalman's Home. She stands on the steps for a while, listening to the roar of the traffic, the hurried footfalls on the pavement, the wail of a siren on Hospital Hill. Then she turns and looks into the vestibule. The Christ-figure is staring into the street, sad-eyed, helpless, crucified on a tapestry of felt.

THREE

Ruth watches the black-collared barbet jab fiercely at the iced-over bird bath which does not yield to his beak. Above him, in the tamarisk tree, his mate sinks her beak into the pawpaw Ruth has impaled on a twig. Eyes shut, feathers puffed, she throws back her head, swallowing a morsel. Every day they come, to drink, to eat, then fly off to the bottom of the garden where they call, kwakaroo, kwakaroo, kwakaroo, seventeen or eighteen times, one singing kwa, the other karoo, in such perfect harmony, it could be one bird calling. They eat here but sing elsewhere, Ruth muses; like everyone else in this household.

It is cold in the study despite the pale sunlight which filters through the Yesterday, Today and Tomorrow. Through its sparse winter foliage, she sees untidy sparrow nests whose occupants hop over the frosted lawn, pecking at breadcrumbs, while bulbuls and mousebirds move in on the pawpaw, serrating it with eager beaks. The shadows of the fir trees, etched in frost, melt at the edges, blurring their sharpness, and the tulip magnolia is about to burst into bloom. Spring: what will she do with spring? Go on a pilgrimage? Write of roots pierced by showers, the engendering of flowers? She feels sapless, dry, and

17

yet she aches to sing. Words. Where can the words be? She takes her diary out of the drawer.

'3 September 1979,' she writes. 'Words, words, words. Where can the words be? Elsewhere. Not in the keyboard, nor in the trees, the shrubs, the birdsong. Elsewhere: off the koppie and over the golf course, past the Homes and across the veld, due north to the township on the verge of the suburbs. That's where the words lie. In the dust of rutted roads, on rubbish heaps where goats feed, in gullies flowing with filth, on the tongues and in the hearts of its denizens. It is their lives, their words. In my hands they jangle like counterfeit. I'll have to tell another tale, sing a different song; probe the abyss between hilltop and hovel and dredge the river between them; mine the rocks, comb the bush, and hunt down the words, all spent and stale, which may still have life in them. But if there's no response, no echo? Then it's too late for words. Where the words lie. Words lie...'

There it is again: kwakaroo, kwakaroo, kwakaroo ... She puts her diary into the drawer and goes to the window.

"Sara!" Ruth cries out as a pair of arms encircle her waist. "You startled me!"

"How'd you know it's me?"

"Who else? Your father isn't playful, Avi's arms aren't long enough, and in the twenty years Selina's worked here, we've hardly touched. Strange, isn't it?"

"Is it?" Sara slackens her hold but does not release Ruth. "She's hardly touched me since I've grown up."

She would snuggle up against Selina's back, enfolded in a blanket tied over her ample breasts, and listen to the hum of her words and her songs, breathing in the warmth of her body and the smell of plain soap and sweat.

Sara places her head against Ruth's back: cool, boney, scented, familiar without evoking childhood. She whirls Ruth around and kisses her on the forehead, ashamed of her disloyalty. Her green eyes sparkle with golden lights as the sun slants through the fir trees.

Ruth's heart contracts with love, with regret. She holds Sara close, smells the fragrance of her skin, feels her long blond hair

18

against her cheek. Then she straightens her arms and with her hands on Sara's shoulders, looks at her: She has Ruth's wide-set eyes, Daniel's eyebrows; her cheekbones, his pale complexion; her slimness, his posture; her mouth, his smile. A physical equivalent of everything their marriage should have been, a blending of their best features. Avi, on the other hand, is his own man, physically and mentally; a throwback to some dark Tartar ancestor who roamed the Russian steppes: a loner.

"Have you finished packing?" she asks Sara.

"Almost. There's not much cupboard space in those old mine houses, so I've made a careful selection."

The old mine houses. Ruth's friend Mavis had lived in one, at the edge of the veld, near the mine: Corrugated iron roof, small windows facing onto a narrow stoep, three tiny bedrooms, and a living room with a fire place; wooden strip floors and pressed iron ceilings. Ruth had lived on the other side of the mine, on the far side of the veld, in a larger house. As soon as they could afford it, her parents, like the other immigrants, had moved out of the mining suburbs, over the koppies into the orange brick suburbs.

And now their descendants were moving back into the mining suburb in the south, closing the circle.

"Why that area, why those houses?" Ruth asks, knowing the answer, knowing also that Sara and her friends cannot expiate the sins of their forebears by living in communes in working-class suburbs. They may escape the opulence, the privileged lifestyle for a while, but they remain white, middle-class students whose parents' tainted money sees them through university and whose maids still do their laundry. Rich Rags they call their faded jeans with a precise understanding of the trap they are struggling to break out of.

"I've told you. They've stopped mining in that area," Sara says, "and the houses are empty. Students moved in some years ago and there's an active community life. Nice mixture of people. Vegetarians and basket weavers, feminists and potters, workerists and populists, and even a few genuine workers. You know, the alternative life-style rubbing elbows with the radical lefties."

19

"How many of you will share the house?"

"Three. Laura, Marlene and myself. We each want a room of our own." She catches Ruth's eye and smiles. "We're bourgeois enough to value privacy. Solitude, not loneliness. You think we're playing at being poor, don't you? Perhaps. But there are some white working-class families living there, and even, dare I whisper it, a few blacks. The real thing, you know. Does that pre-empt your criticism?"

"If you understand this, why are you moving out?"

"We've been over all that before."

"I should've been a full-time mother," Ruth says. "Instead I went to University, painted, wrote, protested, advised. First Avi goes, then you. I'm a failed mother."

"Breast-beater." Sara holds her so tightly that Ruth gasps for breath. She loosens her hold and they sit down on the sofa, laughing. "I remember taking two rand to school in lieu of a cake for the Fête. My mum's writing an essay on T. S. Eliot, I told old Horwitz proudly; she hasn't got time to bake."

"I never went to afternoon lectures," Ruth says, "I'd rush home and try to look as though I'd done nothing all day but wait for your return from school. I couldn't have managed without Selina, of course."

"Of course," Sara says, then discards her sardonic tone. "I realise now what a schlep it must have been: music lessons, speech classes, ballet, tennis coaching, swimming practice. All of which left me totally unscathed. Jis lissen to my South Efriken eksent. But take heart, Mother. Avi may still swim the Channel, become a concert guitarist, or a newsreader on BBC. If he can spare the time from his epidemiology. What do you really think – will he come back to South Africa?"

"Not while he's got an army call-up. But he always said he'd work in Zimbabwe or Maputo if he can't come home again."

"I miss having him around, if only to fight with. The house feels empty without him."

"Imagine how much emptier," Ruth begins. Sara interrupts.

"Let live, loz leben, laat lewe. You've been quite good at it, so don't let old age change you." Sara laughs as she tousles

Ruth's hair, auburn, shot through with grey. "How's the work going? I haven't heard that tap-tap-tap this morning."

"I can't get started. Plenty of ideas but no words." Ruth points to the blank sheet in her typewriter.

"Perhaps your imagination needs to lie fallow for a season. Take a break. Go back to painting for a while."

"I can't. It's those voices, hammering to be let out..."

"Ahah, Mrs Singer. You hear voices?"

"Yes, doctor. Only they're not the voices of immigrants with their familiar accents and obsessions. These are the voices of black people in the townships and in the rural areas. But I can't catch the words, I don't understand their meaning. I only feel the pain."

"I see why Avi and I opted for the sciences, if you can call medicine a science. Perhaps it was my reaction to all those galleries, exhibitions and concerts you dragged us to, and to your constant injunction to read. I'm not complaining. I'm sure it was educational even if it bored us, me anyway, to extinction at the time. But look at Avi. He's quite civilised. Goes to concerts, plays classical guitar and is politically involved. If you failed, you only failed with me. I'm a barbarian."

"You're lucky. You didn't trust me; Avi did. And you're the happier person. It's that mother-daughter thing. I avoided making my mother's mistakes but I made plenty of my own."

"I suppose I am more like Dad; practical. He'd have made a good doctor. He's so calm and reassuring. But it's you I talk to, so don't fret!"

Calm and reassuring. Ruth massages Sara's icy feet gently. Not in front of the children, had been her plea.

"What else did you react against, now that we're being so frank?" she asks. "I keep discovering how little I really know my children."

"If it's going to upset you, I'm not talking."

"Not at all. I'm fascinated. Imagine me saying to my mother, Ma, did you really hate me as a child, or was it just my oedipal hang-ups? Oedipal, schmoedipal ... By the way, Sara, I found that note tucked away in Jock of the Bushveld. 'I hate my fucken mother. I love Daddy.'"

"So, my spelling wasn't very good."

"Little girls always prefer their fathers."

"I'm a big girl now and Dad and I argue about almost everything these days. Besides, I was only seven when I wrote it and I was angry and confused because you'd refused to take us to the circus. It's cruel to train wild animals, you said. Yet you read us stories about animals that talked, sang, built houses or huffed and puffed them down. Now, suddenly, it was cruel to make them leap through a hoop or walk on their hind legs. And that was only one of the contradictions."

"Tell Mummy everything, dear."

"I don't trust your honeyed tones. They sheathe the claws of retribution. How's that for a mixed-up metaphor? You can use it in your next book."

"Who's got the claws?"

"Come, come, Mother. You're always saying what monsters writers are, turning people into characters."

"You make me feel like a literary Medusa. Tell me about the contradictions."

"Contradictions. There we were, living in this beautiful low-slung house of rock, wood, glass and thatch, unobtrusive on the koppie, in very good taste, so comfortable, so safe, with you and Dad agonising about poverty, injustice, discrimination. And right in your backyard was the third world in the shape of two small rooms in one of which Selina and little Luke lived, and in the other Phineas and his wife, sharing a small bathroom and toilet. We went to the best schools, and their children went to mission schools out in the gramadoelas where they lived in unbelievable squalor. Dormitories smelling of stale urine, mealie meal served out of tin baths..."

"We tried to get them into schools in town," Ruth says quietly "but at that time they wouldn't take blacks..."

"I know. Now. But how could Luke have understood? Even now. He'd been born in our backyard, considered himself one of the family. Don't worry, Ma'am, he said when you were looking for schools for him. I'll go to school with Avi and Sara. He probably expected to have a barmitzvah when he turned thirteen. I can't forget his traumatised face when he came back on his first school holiday. Should we be surprised at how he's turned out? We provided the expectations, then dropped him back into the squalor."

Ruth says nothing. She feels a dull familiar ache whenever she thinks about Luke.

"...idealism, politics. I'd seen how they had hurt you, how helpless you were, how ineffectual. So I decided to take a short cut, to forget the grand solutions and do what I could."

"It's difficult to find solutions when you're part of the problem," Ruth says.

"Are there solutions? I'm interested in people, not The People. I remember a character in one of your books who says something about loving the masses and hating people. See, I have learned something from you!"

Ruth puts her arms around Sara and holds her close.

"I'll miss you," she mumbles into Sara's neck.

"For goodness' sake! I'll be ten or twelve kilometres away. I'm not leaving the country. And I'll be bringing my washing home. Listen. Get yourself another dog and I promise, you won't miss me one bit. Dogs don't answer back, smoke pot or play pop music. And they love those who feed them, unconditionally. You've mourned for poor old Caesar long enough. The Alsatian's dead, long live the new dog! I'll go to the pound myself and find a pooch for you. No thoroughbreds with dysplasia this time."

Relieved at the shift in conversation, Ruth says, "Have you heard Dad's new joke? When does life begin? At conception, says the Catholic. At birth, says the Protestant. When the dog dies and the children leave home, says the Jew. So, Sara, go in good health and a new life will begin for us. What kind of life is another matter, of course. Stop giggling. What sort of mother am I if I can't elicit a soupçon of guilt from you?"

"What's a soopsawn? Speak English. I'm illiterate in a dozen languages."

"A minute quantity of something. I'm becoming like some-one I used to know. She larded her speech with French words because between Pinsk and Pofadder, her mother had given birth to her in Paris, where she lived till the age of two."

"I know who you're talking about! Lola Stern. What happened between us and the Sterns? All I know is that when we were kids, we were either at their house or they were at ours. Then all contact ended and we never saw them again. The girls were older than me but I remember that horrible Michael who used to pull my hair. What's the story? You said you'd tell me when I was older. I'm older. Twenty is old, the oldest I've been."

Ruth laughs, disentangles herself from Sara and stands up.

"Some other time. You're packing, Dad's got an early appointment and I've got a heavy day ahead, crowned by a meeting with the writers' group this evening."

"That's why you've got this block," Sara says. "You've been brainwashed by that group into thinking that whites can't write about blacks or that they shouldn't, even if they could."

"Are you going to be a psychoanalyst when you grow up?"

"Got you on a sensitive spot, hey? That's when you start pulling age on me. And where's that manuscript you won't submit because it portrays black characters? I want to read it."

"Take it, it's there, in that red file. And when you're finished, burn it."

"I'll pack it in with my clothes. And I won't burn it," she says, taking the file off the shelf.

"You'd do me a favour if you did. Listen!" Ruth holds up her hand and goes to the window, motioning Sara to join her. "The black-collared barbet. That's the real sound of Africa."

"Bull. That's just a bird warning others not to poach on his territory or he'll tear them to shreds. Perhaps that is the real sound of Africa. I must finish packing. See you at breakfast."

She leaves such silence behind her, Ruth thinks, as Sara goes out of the study.

The household is beginning to stir. A toilet flushes, the shower draws hot water from the tank, and Selina is rattling crockery in the kitchen. Phineas, dressed in blue overalls, with a knitted cap pulled over his eyebrows, leaves footprints in the frost as he walks to the birdbath and empties it with one sweep of his hand, throwing the ice on to the lawn. Watering can in hand, he slouches to the tap. He disapproves of Ruth feeding the birds. "You calling them," he has told her, "and they eat my flowers." That is true. The mousebirds are particularly destructive. But if you want barbets, crested or black-collared, you must put up with mousebirds.

"Ruth!" Daniel calls as he walks along the passage towards the study. "Are you coming for breakfast?"

He is aging well, Ruth thinks as he comes into the study. His blond hair is greying and has that powdered look Avi's had when he played Julius Caesar in his matric year.

"What are you looking at? Have I got toothpaste on my chin?"

"No. I was thinking that if you wore a toga instead of that three-piece suit, you'd look like a Roman senator."

"I might do that. Perhaps that'll raise a laugh at the board meeting. The production results won't. Don't wait for supper. There'll be drinks after the meeting."

"I'm going to a meeting of the writers' group," she says.

"Parallel lives. But it's working, isn't it?"

She smiles but does not answer. In the few seconds they look at one another, she sees the lengthening jowls in his clean-shaven face, the bags under his eyes. He sees the crows' feet at the side of her eyes, the lines bracketing her mouth. They read the past in one another's faces and are reluctant to jettison it.

"By the way." His jowls drop, his lips draw into a thin line. The Roman senator is aggrieved. "I caught Luke sneaking into the backyard last night. I've told Selina a hundred times I'll not have that tsotsi on my premises."

"Our premises. Selina lives here too, and he comes to visit his mother. He was born here."

"Ungrateful little bugger. After all we've done for him. Nothing but a loafer and a thief. Who else could have stolen my watch? He's got free access to the house."

"Daniel, not today. Sara's leaving…"

"Let's invite Luke to move into her room. Maybe Selina would then show more interest in her job. She takes advantage of you. In the factory everyone has fixed hours, knows his job and works the required time…"

"This is not a factory, and you are not our Managing Director. Selina comes in early and works till after dinner. She's entitled to several hours break during the day."

"Just look at those cobwebs."

"Don't take out your frustration with work…"

"There's no point talking to you. I never get support for what you know are perfectly legitimate complaints."

When he leaves the study, she opens the window and a stream of cold air rushes in. Above the chirping of the sparrows, the chatter of the mynahs and cooing of the doves, she hears the barbets again, singing their song, elsewhere.

FOUR

15 October 1979

My dearest Jeanne,

At last, a letter from you. I don't ask much, just a postcard now
and then to say you're well. I did not say you were anorexic: I
said anorexia nervosa seemed to be an occupational hazard
with ballet dancers. Why are mothers always misunderstood?
I'm only starting to understand my own mother now. Don't
you wait that long; let it happen in my lifetime.

I'm sure you'll be happier in the North, without Clive. As
you know, I never liked him much. He was too much of the bon
vivant; all stomach, no heart. I can't imagine ... Uh, uh, I think
I've done it again; I've just pictured your face cramping up with
impatience. Anyway, keep writing. Entre nous, our phone bill
was horrendous last month; I paid it without showing it to
Dad. Chantal isn't much of a writer either, and as it takes
anything up to two weeks for letters between Johannesburg
and Sydney, we don't hear regularly from her, so I phone.

Dad and Michael are well, but never en rapport. I wish they
wouldn't fight so much. Every time Michael brings his laundry
home – one can hardly call it a visit – he and Dad get involved

27

in a political argument. They're so alike, though neither of them sees it. Pity Michael couldn't have known Dad as a young man; they'd have got on well. Zalman's okay but I keep getting phone calls from the Director telling me what a disruptive element he is in the Home. I know he's unhappy there and I do feel a little guilty about it, but it wouldn't work if he came to live with us.

I'm well, but overweight. Food is so comforting. (And there I was, a few paragraphs back, criticising Clive!) I must take myself in hand. I'd reached the stage a few weeks ago when I couldn't bear to go in to the Advice Office. I offered, instead, to do the correspondence at home. We get masses of letters from all over the country. Many of them are smuggled out of prisons and we can't reply to them without getting the prisoners into trouble. Only when they send the name and address of a relative, can we ask the Legal Resources Centre to act on their behalf. Most letters are filed away with the comment, 'nothing can be done'. They're usually from what is known as the 'criminal' element, not political detainees, most of whom claim to be innocent, many of whom probably are. One imagines them sitting there, waiting for us to DO something. I sometimes wonder if I shouldn't have stuck it out in the office. The picture of the prisons that emerges is horrific. It's another world, ruled by warders and gangsters, a microcosm of the world outside. Every time I fetch the mail, that Christ figure on the tapestry I told you about, seems to reproach me. Not my fault, I mutter, averting my eyes. But I'm not so sure. Let me give you some idea of the sort of letter we have to handle. Most of the writers don't know what our organisation is about. They've heard from other people that we advise those in need, so they write to these anonymous 'helpers'.

Honourable Madams,
I'm the above-mentioned person. Hereby lodge my complain to your table and I pray to God you'll do be kind and put your keen eye to it. I was convicted for housebreaking and robbery of wich I never commit. We were two accuses in this case...

Dear Madems,
I saw a doctor surgery in 1975 August and I was well according to the doctor's post mortem stating that I am physically feet and healthy...

Mr Sir Presithenthir,
Greetins are the opening of my correspondence. I start first asking how is all the family in the house? I aply to you who may accept it...

I'm claiming about being injure in maximum prison. I never received money of being injure. They only had sent me for extrey. After been extreid there were no other effort was taken ... The whole leg started to swell up. I have tried to report so many times to authorities of the prison, they just ignor me, they say I'm pretending there is no such thing like that. More over they sent me to the work of carpentry though my leg is swollen if I complain they promise me to lock up in this single cell. I should be happy if my application may be acceptable and considerable. As I request, your faithful.

Dear Madams,
We are hereby asking aid from you and your Noble Body to assist us about the above prison as we are heaving some unsolved problems ... Honourable madams, we are complaining about food we are eating in this prison. It is too little than before. The Captain ... mention that this prison uses its own law. And there's no transfer...

Dear Madam,
We have requested various authorities for supreme solution to our father. He is serving the imprisonment term of four years for capable homicide which he unexpected committed ... In the prison he was assaulted by a warder and the pain has become more severe. While the warder was busy assaulting him the warder was using abusive language. My father told the sergeant in question that he is going to lay a charge against him for assaulting him. The warder's reply was that he is a prisoner

similar to a dog, a useless creature. He can report wherever he wanted but he was confident nobody would listen to his complaint...

Your Excellency,
In first degree respect I the above mentioned am a black old woman of 77 years of age. I am a Mother parent of six children but my first born is convicted. He is serving the penal of nine to fifteen imprisonment ... So I, the above mentioned Mother of the so-called convict here by wish to submit my request before your Excellency in order to gane more help from your Honoured views of help ... Now I'm in the great dilma ... Please help me, for I'm too old to travel from here in Pretoria to the distanity and farness of Barberton Prison ... I hope you will be of great help to me...

And so on, Jeanne. Most letters are written on scraps of paper, on the back of telegram forms, or on anything that presents a blank surface. Some have obviously been written by a prison scribe whose style you begin to recognise. Mary, the woman with whom I trained in the Advice Office, has asked me to keep records of the letters. We hope to hand them over to lawyers who may come up with a way of helping. Very difficult, as it is illegal to publish anything about prisons. Be well. Love from all, and do write soon. Even a few words.
    Love, Ma

FIVE

As Ruth walks into the *Skelm* office, she is reminded of the old
Movement house in Doornfontein. WORKERS OF THE WORLD
UNITE! a clenched white fist had ordered from a dog-eared
graphic on a peeling wall. Here a black fist demands POWER!
Then, the blue-shirted chaverim – the nearest translation is
comrades – had been white; now the comrades are black. The
prophets, except one or two, are different. So are the heroes.
And the rousing Cossack rhythms and Slavic melodies have
been replaced by African drums. But the underlying assumption
remains: it is possible and necessary to change the world.

The *Skelm* office is messy. Desks and work-benches are
littered with manuscripts, paste-ups and galleys. The walls are
hung with drawings and photographs which have appeared in
Skelm, the magazine which Nicholas brings out: bulldozers
demolishing squatter camps; policemen charging a crowd of
demonstrators with batons and tear gas; a man carrying the
limp body of a boy. Black victims of a vicious system. Ruth
wonders if the cover picture on the first issue of *Skelm* – black
people penned behind a barbed wire fence – had been interpreted

as a deliberate echo of the Nazi era. The Publications Control Board had banned it on sight.

Ruth had gone to her first meeting in that old house in Doornfontein just after World War II. At eighteen, she had felt the need to commit herself to a cause, to enter the bloodstream of History. But to which cause, to whose history? Should she fight racism at home, in Africa, or should she help create a new society on the kibbutz? Not for a moment had she doubted the attainability of either ideal: after the war everything seemed possible. Humanity was being given another chance, its last perhaps, to create a better world. It was simply a matter of which path to take. If you will it, one of her culture heroes had said, it is no dream.

On that particular evening, Ruth could not have known she would never live on a kibbutz, but even then she had had misgivings about her fellow Utopians. They were young and bright-eyed, idealistic and pure. They were also rigid and judging, the self-appointed keepers of the Only Truth. Paul had come towards her saying, I'm pleased you've come. I hope you will join us. He never made it to the kibbutz either.

A few weeks ago she had driven through Doornfontein. All the houses have been razed, and in their place stand large office blocks and a technical college. She had not even found the street where the house had stood.

As for racism ... A luta continua, the activists say. Ruth feels too weary, too wary, for another struggle.

Nicholas, who insists he is not the editor of *Skelm* – it is brought out by an editorial collective – detaches himself from an earnest young man in a corner, and comes towards her.

"I'm pleased you've come," he says.

Again the déjà vu. But he is fair, short and wiry, walks fast and talks fast. Paul had been – is, for all she knows, she hasn't seen him in fifteen years – tall and dark, and used to enunciate each syllable clearly. Momen-ta-rily, she remembers him saying in some forgotten context. The high cheekbones? Paul's originated in the Russian steppes; Nicholas' in the Celtic highlands. The charisma? She hesitates to use the word. These days it is attributed to anyone with appeal; it no longer evokes the image of a divinely inspired individual who elicits devotion and enthusiasm from his or her followers. According to Sara, even pop stars have it. What such disparate people do have in common, is harmony with the spirit of their times – and the young, seeking expression for their own aspirations, recognise this. They hurl themselves into the wake of these shooting stars and are borne along rapturously until they are burned out, dizzy with the illusion that they had actually been going somewhere. She had seen this happen to Paul; she hopes Nicholas will be spared. At the moment he is right on course.

Paul had been a student of anthropology, a Zionist-Marxist – a political aberration, the new radicals would call him, a centaur-like throwback to mythical times – who had been swept by the Zeitgeist almost to the gates of the kibbutz. No one quite recovers from such a journey. Vestigial yearnings still surface in her from time to time, but she has learned to keep them in check. Living with Daniel helps. He discarded – or suppressed – his millenarian longings many years ago.

As she watches the young blacks around Nicholas, her heart aches for them: they believe implicitly in the power of the word. With poems written on the backs of cigarette boxes, with the incantations chanted before eager audiences, with their plays and their stories, they hope to bring down the walls of Jericho. They know their struggle cannot be won with words alone, but for now it is their only weapon, their sole consolation. And they trust Nicholas, himself a poet, whose genius is perfect pitch: he has tuned in to the chorus of black voices which sing out their people's grief and anger in the aftermath of the '76 Rebellion, and he is reproducing it, note-perfect, in *Skelm,* which he has made their mouthpiece. But he himself no longer writes poetry: it is not my song, he says when Ruth remonstrates with him over his silence. This, perhaps, is why they trust him.

Nicholas speaks loudly to make himself heard above the drums which Mandla Magwaza is beating with his open palms as he recites, "...little Hector died, and Africa went on mourning..." Mandla is surrounded by a small group which listens in respectful silence. His epic poem, a best-seller in the townships, has recently been banned. Ruth has heard him read excerpts from it to black audiences who join in the chorus, acclaiming him as he strides across the platform in his flowing robes: "Africa my beginning," they chant with him, "and Africa my ending."

"As you see," Nicholas says, "very few white writers have pitched up. Their enthusiasm for a non-racial writers' group seems to have evaporated."

"They were keen enough in the beginning," Ruth says. "but they've been discouraged. They went to poetry readings in the townships, they offered to run workshops for the young black writers..."

"Such arrogance! Theirs, not yours," Nicholas hastens to assure her. "Workshops aren't run, one participates in them. Our white intellectuals haven't understood a thing, least of all the emergence of a new kind of literature that's inspired by music, by the oral tradition, and by the common experience of poet and people. Our white writers sit in their ivory towers and are appalled by the tortured syntax, the fractured grammar. They're itching to sanitise this spontaneous outburst of song and protest, to impose their 'standards' on it. But you've heard me sound off on this before. Can you stay after the meeting? There's something I'd like to discuss with you."

Ruth nods assent, smiling. Nothing changes; one does not talk, one discusses. But Nicholas is right, of course. This is what she has been agonising over in her own ivory tower. The blacks know where the words lie. The words may be raw, the phrases flawed, the ideas naive, but that too tells a tale. It may not even be literature. But does it matter? The room vibrates with the sound of drums which seem to devour Mandla's words. She no longer knows whether it matters or not.

David knows. He is standing next to Mandla, trying to hear the words behind the drums. To him it matters. He understands this experiment in openness, the popular character of the new writing that is bursting out of the townships. He sees how it fits with the African oral tradition, and understands how the

34

readings work as political consciousness-raising rituals. But he will not compromise on standards. Let us have workshops, he urges at every meeting. They will not inhibit what the black writers have to say; they will only sharpen their weapons. But workshops remain a thorny issue.

David smiles at her. Their friendship dates back to the early fifties, when she and Daniel had returned from Israel, forlorn and disillusioned. Back 'home', they had been swept up into an unending round of dinner parties which did nothing to relieve the shock of their return. At one of these parties they had met David and his wife Rina. He was a large, shaggy man with a mop of red hair, and Rina was small, neat and dark. "What am I supposed to do with this?" he had asked Ruth in a mock whisper when a finger bowl with a slice of lemon draped over the edge was placed in front of him; "Drink it?" "Don't mind him," Rina had said briskly. "He's totally unsocialised." "He's a famous poet," the hostess excused him. "If I'm so famous," David had said, chewing the twist of lemon, "how come I need an introduction?" His eyes twinkled under his bushy eyebrows as he turned to Ruth. They took to one another immediately. "I am a full-time English teacher," he told her, "who writes poetry only when I can't help it." "I write fiction," she confided. He had invited her to join a writers' circle and nursed her through the frustrating early years of her writing career. She had met Nicholas through David.

"By the way," Ruth says to Nicholas, "I spoke to Daniel about Vusi. He has a job for him."

"Great. We'll talk to Vusi after the meeting."

A slim young man with large glasses and a shy smile offers Ruth his chair. She demurs but takes it when he settles down on the tacky carpet. A few months ago Nicholas had introduced him to her as "Thami, our Soweto Renaissance man. Not only does he paint, sculpt, write poetry and play the flute and drums, (and the saxophone, Thami had interjected, setting the record straight as he gave her an African handshake – palms, thumbs, palms) but he is also one of the *Skelm* team that keeps in touch with writers' groups throughout the country. He'll go far,"

Nicholas had added as Thami moved away. "Not into exile, I hope," Ruth had said. Nicholas had drawn his eyebrows together and pursed his mouth.

Like the chaverim, he did not realise it was permissible, even essential, to laugh at one's sorrows. A *bittere gelechter,* bitter laughter, her forebears had called it; the healing laughter that assuages pain.

What graceful, slender hands Thami has. Ruth looks around the room. Like Joshua's, like Masilo's, like Vusi's. She wonders if Verwoerd had looked at the long, tapering fingers and smooth knuckles of the blacks before assigning them to be hewers of wood and drawers of water. He probably had, with envy and fear.

There are few women in the room: Ma-Deborah, a large, good-looking woman in her forties, is a novelist whose only book has been banned. She had referred to the Afrikaners as 'bloody Boere.' She is sitting next to a young actress who also writes poetry. Ruth knows her only as Nkatsana. Jenny, Nicholas' editorial assistant, sits on the other side of Nkatsana. Jenny is English, in her mid-twenties and has a pleasant gamine-type face with a wide smile which, however, she reserves for blacks and a few favoured whites. She is dressed in grubby jeans and a creased Indian cotton shirt. Despite the cold, she is wearing sandals through which dirty toenails protrude. She is paging through *Spare Rib* with Nkatsana.

"The black woman," she is saying, "is at the bottom of the pile. Not only is she subject to all the oppressive legislation that applies to all blacks; she is also a perpetual minor in the laws of her own people. Yet she's the one who carries the can, who's responsible for the whole family. The struggle begins at home."

"I hear what you're saying," Nkatsana passes her hand over the plaits which cover her gleaming scalp in a geometric design, "but the Struggle comes first. Then we'll start on our male chauvinist pigs." She laughs as she cuffs Thami gently on the head. She sews her own clothes and always looks immaculate. Tonight she is wearing a brown German-print dress with white flowers.

Jenny catches Ruth's eye and greets her, unsmiling. Ruth is not a favoured white. She writes 'irrelevant' fiction, none of which has ever been banned, about a privileged section of the community.

There are two Indian writers and a 'coloured' poet amongst the blacks. Ruth wonders if they, too, feel excluded by language, education and privilege. Cassim is a doctor, Ebrahim is a teacher, and Willie is a student who has recently come up from the Cape. There are such subtle gradations of privilege among them, that Ruth fears the gossamer thread of literature will not hold them together.

Mandla puts aside the drums and his audience begins to talk animatedly amongst themselves in Sotho – or is it Zulu? Although the discussion is obviously serious, short bursts of laughter punctuate the cross current of conversation. She wishes she understood what they were saying; she has never learned a Bantu language. What she does recognise, however, is the bright-eyed earnestness, the certainty.

Another time, another cause: hope seems to reincarnate itself in the young. She is grateful it exists somewhere.

There is one older writer among them: Simon Sibandla. He gives Ruth a cold smile which she returns with an added measure of ice. Opportunist, she mutters to herself. He had once been a Congress supporter. Now he has jumped on to the Black Consciousness bandwagon, apparently the dominant ideology in the townships these days. She expects him to turn full circle if circumstances change. Despite the disdainful pose he strikes in the presence of whites, and the scathing articles he writes for the newspaper he works on, he still goes to dinner parties in the Northern suburbs. He sleeps through most of these meetings, his double chin resting on the embroidered collar of his tunic, his hands folded over his paunch. He is quite a good writer, she concedes, but his recent poems have an unattractive strident tone. One simulates the sound of an AK47 – 'kak-kak-kak-kak-kak'. But at least she has his measure. Mogorosi, who is now speaking softly to Nicholas, is an enigma to her. He has a lean and hungry look, she decides, and wonders who or what it is that he is set on devouring.

"I think we should start," Nicholas says when Mogorosi sits back, his face impassive, his arms folded. "Thami is chairman tonight."

"First," Thami takes out some crumpled notes from his checked pants, "I will give you news about the groups. Then we must talk about the censorship and banning problem."

Gartasso, Guyo, Abangani, Zamani, Khauleza, he reels off the names of some of the groups in every corner of the country. Bayajula, Mpumalanga, Mbakasima, Kwanza ... They send in poems and stories from their members and Thami, Nicholas and Mogorosi make selections from them for *Skelm*. They would like to publish everything, but space is limited. Thami keeps contact with the groups, gives encouragement, and consoles the rejected. Have readings amongst yourselves, he urges them. Workshop your writing together. Workshop is the buzzword; it is only in this milieu that it has become a sensitive issue.

"Bad news, bad news on the censorship and banning front," Thami says. "Seven black writers in detention, eight writers have been banned, and five have been refused passports. We have taken statements from six writers who have recently suffered harassment from the police. All of them black. But they have also banned a novel by Jan de Villiers, the Afrikaans writer. As you know, Vusi here has just been sentenced to one year's imprisonment, suspended for five years, just for being in possession of the Freedom Charter."

Thami adds something in the vernacular and there is a roar of laughter among the blacks. Ruth guesses it has to do with the fact that as a supporter of Black Consciousness, he does not accept the Freedom Charter as a bill of rights. The anomaly appeals to the audience. Good sign; they are beginning to laugh at their troubles.

"And the magistrate," Nicholas adds, "said that he had read the Charter and found it contained nothing seditious. But his duty, he said, was to implement the laws of the State, not to question them. Sorry, Thami, carry on."

"Ja," Thami says. "The harassment of black writers is increasing. And they stop us from selling *Skelm* in the townships. They arrested the guy who sells them outside Mofifi's fish and chips shop. He always shouts, 'Knowledge! Knowledge! Come fetch your *Skelm* from here!' Mogorosi has written a letter to the Commissioner of Police on behalf of the writers' group."

Thami reads the letter. Mogorosi sits silently, his arms crossed, listening. Ruth recognises Nicholas' style.

"A poem is not a gun." There is a murmur of approval as one of the phrases in the letter is repeated throughout the room. "Hai man, that's good," someone says. "A poem is not a gun. Hai!"

Vusi then tells them how a group of about ten policemen interrogated him, making him stand through hours of questioning. They asked him about the membership of the writers' group, how often they met, and with which other groups they were affiliated. "Then this Lieutenant Van Wyk who pretended to be the good one and who stopped the others from hitting me, told me to stop writing and to stop distributing *Skelm*, because that will put me in trouble. He also said it was a silly way for a man to make a living. He said I wouldn't earn good money."

"For sure you won't," David says wryly. Everyone laughs. David is universally loved. In spite of a heavy work schedule at school and very little time in which to write his own poetry, he has never turned away any young writer who has sought his help or advice. "And talking about writing, when are we going to discuss workshops?" he asks. "I'm getting to be a bore on the subject, I know, but we must make a start."

"We're drafting a questionnaire which we'll print in the next issue of *Skelm*, asking what kind of workshop the writers would like," Nicholas says hurriedly. "We'll submit the draft to the next meeting."

It takes some time for everyone to drift away when the meeting ends. Ruth goes over to the drums and tentatively taps out a rhythm – tum tudarantum, tum-tum. It emits a soft, hollow sound. Encouraged, she relaxes her wrists and tries something a little more ambitious. Her movements aren't sharp enough and a muffled hum emerges through the cowskin hide.

"Like this," Vusi says, coming up to the drums, and once again the drums speak in familiar rhythms. Nicholas is right; it is their song.

"Vusi," she says, "there's a job at the factory. Nothing marvellous, but at least you'll be earning a reasonable salary."

"In the factory?" Vusi looks distressed.

"It's in the office," she explains, "to help with the invoicing and the filing."

Vusi looks down at the floor and says nothing.

Nicholas, a little embarrassed, says, "Um, yes. What Vusi would really like to do is to work on *Skelm*. He is writing very good poems, you know. But unfortunately we just haven't got enough money for another salary. What will he be earning, if he takes the job?"

"About four hundred rand a month."

Nicholas laughs. "That's more or less what I'm earning at the moment. Well, Vusi, how do you feel about it?"

"I, well, you know, Nicholas. The money's okay." He looks at Ruth, then drops his eyes again. "Man, it's soul-destroying, working in industry."

Ruth takes a deep breath but says nothing. This is one conversation she will not repeat to Daniel. He says thanks, Daniel, but he's already found a job.

"It's not in the factory," Nicholas says. "It's in the office."

"Well, yes, man. Perhaps I can just come in to this office and help you with lay-out, Nicholas. And I can help Thami with the groups. You don't have to pay me. Perhaps just bus fare."

Before she can stop herself, Ruth says, "Vusi, what do you live on?"

"Well, I'm at home, in Tembisa, in my mother's house. My father died two years ago."

"How many children are there at home?"

"Four. I'm the eldest. My sisters are still at school."

"And what does your mother do?"

"She does washing, for the white madams in the suburbs."
Vusi looks at her defiantly. Ruth, her conscience stilled for once,
looks right back at him.

"That must be soul-destroying, for her."

"Ruth, can you hang on a minute?" Nicholas looks flus-
tered. "See you tomorrow, Vusi, there's something I have to
discuss with Ruth."

"Sorry," he mutters after Vusi has left the room. "Serves me
right for playing matchmaker or employment bureau or whatever. However hard one tries, one falls into that patronising
role again and again. Thank Daniel from me. Vusi'd obviously
be too unhappy doing clerical work. Perhaps we'll all take a
cut and create another salary for him. Now, about that other
matter. Remember you once offered to do proof-reading and a
bit of editing for *Skelm*? I'd really like to take you up on that
offer. As you know we've no money and I'm literally snowed
under. Jenny can't manage it all, and Thami's English isn't good
enough for subbing. I know you're sensitive to the problems in
black writing and wouldn't rewrite or edit too harshly..."

"I'd be happy to help out," Ruth says. "I write in the
morning, but I could come in, say, three afternoons a week.
Would that be all right? And of course I wouldn't expect to be
paid. I'll take free copies of *Skelm* as wages."

"That's great! There's something else. Our overseas donors
have offered us funds to expand and start publishing books.
Mostly to encourage black writing. It's still in the early stages
but it looks as though it might happen. Isn't that exciting?"

"Sounds wonderful."

"Sorry about Vusi," Nicholas says as he walks to the lift
with her. "But one must understand..."

"Actually I don't understand. What I do know is that revolutions aren't made by elitist elements who write poetry. They
can beat their breasts and their drums and invoke Mother
Azania as much as they like, but real change will only come
through the people who are doing the soul-destroying work."

"Ja, well," Nicholas looks discomfited and Ruth feels
ashamed of her outburst. She smiles at Nicholas as she goes into

41

the lift. "Goodnight, Nicholas, I'll be in on Monday afternoon."

The watchman is standing over his coal brazier, warming his hands as she steps out of the building. "Evening, ma'am," he answers when she bids him good night.

Her anger with Vusi subsides when she thinks about *Skelm*. This will put her in touch with real things, draw her out of her eyrie in the hills. She feels a flutter of excitement; she may even find the right words. As she takes a deep breath, she imagines she smells orange blossoms.

Get thee behind me Satan whose real name is Hope, she thinks as she gets into her car. She is too old and too weary to become involved again.

SIX

3 October 1979

I am too old to be writing in this notebook. What's more, it's becoming a habit, and I need another habit like I need a boil on the tip of my nose – a pristzik auffen shpitz noz. How right that sounds in Yiddish. To think that one day there may be only half a dozen scholars in the world who will be able to decipher such a phrase. I'm always telling you, Lola, that Yiddish is a dying tongue. Nonsense, you say. It is being studied in the universities these days. Exactly, I reply. You look at me blankly. I am very fond of you, Lola, and enjoy visiting you and your family – my watch tells me you are ten minutes late already – but how I wish you had grown up in the shtetl and not in this country. There is a blandness about the higa, the locals; a sharpness, a salti-ness, is missing from their make-up, your make-up. Like Shmuel Leibowitz said when his Christian daughter-in-law converted to Judaism: Jewish she may have become; a Litvak she'll never be.

So I've got this new habit, writing in a notebook. As though I'm not plagued with enough habits: breathing, sleeping, eating, and all those other biological functions which cause such discomfort if they are not properly attended to. What a mensch

43

is reduced to. As you know, I'm not given to casting my eyes skywards and thanking Whoever for allowing me to live and breathe. But when I see those unfortunate creatures in the hospital wards – I only go there when I have to – tethered to the oxygen tanks by long green tubes like dogs to their kennels, I admit to feelings that resemble gratitude. When I reach their stage, I shall take the lift to the top floor – I'd die of heart failure if I tried to walk up those stairs – and throw myself out of a window. With my luck, I'd only break a leg.

The air is full of dust: the rains are late this year. Every day more clouds drift in from the south but dissolve into the flat blue sky without releasing a drop of rain. I sit here in the spring sunshine, waiting for you, and I look across the golf course at the houses on the hill that cling to its sides like ticks on a dog. They enrage me, those houses. Such arrogance. This hill is ours by conquest, they shout, and here we have built our fortresses. Have you noticed, Lola? The walls are growing higher every day.

I am amazed, on reading through this notebook, that I have covered so much ground since I began scratching up the past. In just a few months I have written about my childhood in the shtetl, my departure for the Yeshiva in Kovno, and my banishment from that worthy institution not long afterwards. Excuse for the expulsion: I had tied together the coat-tails of two earnest Yeshiva bocherim as they sat arguing about a passage in the Bible. As they got up to go their separate ways, they found they were bound by more than their religious beliefs. Reason: the Rebbe understood that I was not a Believer, and he was afraid I might infect the others. I do not hold it against him. I'd have made a poor rabbi. As it is, I became a poor tailor. Not because I wasn't good at my work: I was the best apprentice Bere-Yankes ever had. I was so good, in fact, that when I came to this country, I set up an excellent maisterskaya, a workshop to which the richest men flocked. But my excellence was also my downfall. I stuck to my trade while second-rate tailors who made their customers look twisted, shapeless and deformed in the suits they made them, opened sweat-shops and became rich

44

men. Mere tzobbes, that's what they were; they couldn't sew a straight seam.

They only knew how to make trousers. I never envied their wealth; I could not have lived by the sweat of others.

How noble I sound. I am remodelling my character like I used to remodel old suits after my rich customers started buying factory-made clothes. A liar and a hypocrite, that's what I am. I just didn't have the foresight to go into manufacturing. I had no business sense. Had John Sibiya not come towards me at this moment, carrying a fork and a spade, I'd have gone on boasting about how I could never live by the labour of others. Where shall I dig, Mr Zalman, he asks me. Shhh, Mr Sibiya, I say. Not so loud. Let us go around the back of the Home where the land has been set aside for occupational therapy. These two words I have to write in English; which self-respecting Jew knows how to say them in Yiddish? In der heim we either worked so hard that we had no time or need for therapy, or we wore out shoe leather just trying to find an occupation. Therapy? Who needed therapy? You either ran around like a meshugener through the streets, chased by children and dogs, or you were locked up in the madhouse. Therapy. All right, Lola, I'll stop playing the shtetl Jew. But you must admit there is a large element of truth in what I'm saying.

Now that I've shown Mr Sibiya where to dig, let me tell you how it all started, this therapy of theirs. Someone, probably a social worker, had a rush of blood to the head: old people need to feel useful, to be occupied. So the Home is holding a gardening competition, of all things, for the fitter residents, of whom I am judged to be one. Being healthy, as you can see, has its hazards. I don't *need* therapy, I want to yell at them in my usual co-operative manner. While my eyesight holds out, I have my books. But for once I am holding my tongue: I have a plan.

Mr Sibiya, I said to him a few days ago, how would you like to earn some extra money on your day off? On my day off, he said with great dignity, I like to be with my family. He has two sons, two daughters, and a wife. Two of the children, he tells me, are not at home. There is some worry about them, I can see,

45

but of course I respect his desire for privacy. He seems especially proud of one girl. Agnes is very clever, he has told me many times; she will make something of her life. I wouldn't normally try to persuade him about anything he does not wish to do, but this time I really needed his help. It needn't take long, I said. You do the spadework and I'll take over from there. And if we win the prize, we'll share it. So we've come to an understanding, Mr Sibiya and I, though I think he's doing it more to please me than to earn a few extra cents.

I ask you. Gardening. If I had wanted to become a farmer, I'd have joined that rogue Silverman who is called the Potato King, and who has made millions from the labour of slaves and convicts on his farms in the Eastern Transvaal. He once offered me goodness-knows-how-many morgen or hectares or acres, in return for half a dozen suits. Wear potato sacks like your slaves, I told him. Lola, I hear the noble note creeping into my writing again. What is this craving I have for making a better man of myself?

You are still not here. One after another the cars are arriving, driven mostly by young women coming to do their duty by the old ones they've stuck away here. On a Sunday, as one drives through Johannesburg, one sees white heads among the black, brown and blond heads, the old ones being let out on parole for a few hours. Then at five, we are returned to our cells, and the whole city draws a sigh of relief. It's been a strain, listening to the incessant talk of the old, smelling their chicken-hok odour – I smell it myself, in the Home – hearing for the thousandth time the stories about der heim and how good the good old days were – in that mud and slush and poverty and unhappiness. I'm not trying to make you feel guilty, Lola; you owe me nothing. I just don't want to be an object of duty or pity. I never did my duty by anyone, and I don't want anyone to do their duty by me. Perhaps I'm just an ungrateful, cantankerous old man. One good thing about this diary; when something's written down, it's down. I'm not going to apologise or scratch out a single word.

I recognise your car coming up the drive. Yes. And Michael is driving it. I am pleased you have passed on the chore of fetching me on a Sunday to Michael. My heart lifts when I see him. There is something about him that reminds me of myself at the age of twenty. No, I was more worldly wise. He reminds me more of my brother Leib, the idealist. He is a very fine young fellow, Michael. Don't worry about him. He is questioning, looking for a way, though I do worry about that. I think about Leib ... Better than going into his father's business and making money and thinking about nothing else. Not that he'd make money in his father's business ... I go on writing and Michael smiles. He understands. He has kept me waiting and now I keep him waiting. Secret code, hey? he says, looking at the Yiddish writing in the diary. For ignoramuses like you, it's a secret code, I say; for others it is a rich language. I do not add that it is a dying language; he's got his own troubles. He lies down on the grass and looks up at the sky. He's ready when I am. I am very fond of Michael. He doesn't patronise me. So I finish off now because I've kept him waiting long enough.

SEVEN

"Makes you feel snug, secure," Michael says to Zalman as he presses the remote control button and the maws of the garage open quickly, silently, then shut behind them. He parks his mother's Mazda next to a black Mercedes. His own motor bike stands against a wall. "It's all part of the security scene: twenty-four hour patrol, panic buttons, alarm systems, paramedic units. Private armies to protect us from the blacks who, in turn, have the whole of the South African Defence Force protecting them. Zalman, we're in the middle of a civil war, only we haven't given a name to it yet."

"What are you making big speeches for? Keep that for your student newspaper. Your parents had a lot of burglaries, so they got an alarm. Simple. Your father's always flying around and your mother's alone in the house. Who will look after her? Not Jeanne, she's dancing in England. Not Chantal, she's married in Sydney. Not you, you've moved out and are busy making revolutions in Crown Mines."

"Come off it, Zalman. You know they should sell the ancestral home and move into an apartment. They don't need such a mansion. My mother can't seem to break from her childhood. In the townships, half a dozen families would be living in it."

"Never mind. Your sisters have gone. When are you leaving South Africa?"

"I'm staying."

"What about the army?"

"I only get a call-up when my studies are finished. I'll make sure I get well-educated. Then I'll make a plan."

"In the old days, they shot off a toe."

"Thanks for the advice, but I'm rather attached to all the parts of my body."

"You want to be arrested. Look at your shirt."

Michael looks at his shirt. RESIST APARTHEID MILITARISM, he reads the black print on the yellow material. "Strong symbol, that clenched fist. I could've got one with a broken rifle, but this one's more positive."

"You want to be a Yoska Pandarus; you are asking to be hung up. Believe me, the blacks won't thank you for it. Leave me, you trouble maker. I can get out of the car myself. You'll give your mother a heart attack one day."

"Now that you mention it, Zalman, I'm rather worried about my mother. Remember how she steered clear of politics? Well, now she stands on street corners wrapped in a black sash, holding placards that say things like END CONSCRIPTION; CHARGE OR RELEASE DETAINEES; STOP BORDER RAIDS. She goes on protest marches and signs all sorts of petitions. Goodness knows what she'll do next. She'll get into trouble one day. Ah, here she is, come to welcome the prodigal son and uncle. I must tell you, Zalman, she thinks you're a bad influence on me, that I've inherited your, uhm, restless nature. I don't mind, do you? She also thinks insanity is hereditary. You get it from your children, she says, and she's slowly but surely going around the twist."

"Don't make from me an accomplice. Show respect. I'm old enough to be your grandfather."

Michael laughs.

"That's a change," Lola says as she takes Zalman by the arm. "I haven't heard you laugh for a long time."

"You don't make funny remarks," Michael says, bounding up the stairs into the house.

Paul is sitting in the lounge with the Sunday papers spread out in front of him. He threads a hand through his thick dark hair, which is greying at the temples, and acknowledges Zalman with a faint smile. He's getting fat, Zalman notices, and his eyes look tired, puffy. Too many dinners on his expense account, too many late nights. Zalman has never warmed to Paul. He is polite to him for Lola's sake.

"Don't get up," Zalman says as Paul leans back in his chair and yawns. "I don't like fuss."

"Nothing personal, Zalman," Paul says. "I've had a busy week. Malawi, Botswana, Swaziland. Travelling exhausts me."

"I'll never be like my father," Michael has told Zalman. "The big Zionist-Marxist who never made it to the kibbutz, the great anthropologist who is creating a tame workforce for the gold mines." "Don't be so judging," Zalman tells Michael. "Your father helped improve living conditions for the black workers. He can't fight the whole system." "That's what I'm going to do," Michael says, "fight the whole bloody system."

"What do you hear from the girls?" Zalman asks Lola.

He is not really interested. He lost contact with them when they reached their teens; they reminded him too much of his sister Bailka, or Belle, as she renamed herself when she arrived in South Africa. This crazy obsession with names. Good that his own name will die with him; who needs another Zalman in the world? With Lola's collusion, he suspects, Bailka named her older granddaughter Jeanne, after their late father Jankel, and Chantal, the younger one, after their late mother Chana. Zalman cannot imagine how Michael escaped such a fate – not that the name of an archangel is appropriate for such a loafer – but Paul must have put his foot down. One thing about Paul; he has no affectations. And he knew how to handle his rich, arrogant mother-in-law, she should rest in peace. No wonder Bailka/Belle's husband chose an early death; he had fulfilled his mission in life. He made lots of money, bought his wife fur coats and diamonds to wear at her charity functions, then died. A perfect husband.

There are some things, Zalman decides, that he is not going to write in his little black book, not even in Sanskrit. Why upset Lola? She finds her inheritance enough of a burden; she feels guilty about being rich. She could, of course, give it all away, but Lola does not have that kind of courage. She will not deprive her children of their inheritance, nor will she make a Queen Lear of herself. Now that was a writer who understood tragedy. Zalman would have liked to read him in English, but the Russian translation has to do. The Russians also understood tragedy; the real Russians, not the Five Year Planners.

"They're well," Lola says and for a moment Zalman wonders who she is talking about. "Jeanne has dropped ballet and is working with a small modern dance group in Manchester. She still sees that wretched Clive when she goes to London, but I'm hoping distance will cure that. Chantal and Erwin have moved into what they call a terrace house in a place called Paddington. In Australia they love that iron lace, narrow passages and dark rooms that smell of mould. If you saw it, Zalman, you'd place it immediately: Troyeville, Judith Paarl, Bertrams."

Lola sighs and looks out at the garden. The lawn is brown and dry, waiting for the spring rains; the pool shimmers in the clear, crisp air, the shrubs are in bloom, and the flower beds are massed with African daisies, stocks and primulas.

"Nice smells from the kitchen," Zalman says. "Expecting guests?

"Only the four of us."

Zalman is relieved. He loves a quiet Sunday at Lola's house. They sit on chairs under the willow tree, he falls asleep, Lola knits or reads, Paul disappears into his study. If Michael is there with his friends, they swim or lie around in the sun, talking earnestly. T-shirt ideologists, Paul calls them. Unisex. Zalman has to look twice to establish if he is looking at a boy or a girl. He feels strangely moved by them, those eager young people with their hearts on their shirts. But he does not talk to them. Had they understood Yiddish – or Russian or Hebrew, for that matter – they might have had long conversations. Zalman is shy of his accent, his syntax; English must be the most difficult language to learn. And he often does not understand them; everyone speaks so softly these days. Except that stupid Yachna who lives next door to him in the Home. She has a hearing aid but will not use it because she does not want the batteries to wear out. So she shouts because she cannot hear what she is saying.

Zalman sighs. Old people shouldn't be born.

"Are you studying for your exams," he asks Michael, who comes into the lounge carrying a pile of books, "or are you just making weight-lifting?" He lowers his voice. Next thing Lola will buy him a hearing aid.

"I'm studying because I can't afford to fail. The army awaits me."

"At least the army's real," Paul mumbles, "not the Struggle, the System, the People. All cloak, no dagger."

"Paul!" Lola hates it when he belittles Michael's aspirations with slick cynicism. She knows he wants to save him from heartache, but sometimes thinks he is punishing both himself and Michael for a failure in ideology. Michael has no defence against such barbs: At first he took refuge in humour. Now he withdraws in anger and disgust. She is not surprised he left home.

"It's a racist army fighting and destabilising the frontline states, hunting down our own exiles," she says defiantly. She is wary of Paul's amusement at what he calls the radicalisation of Lola S. "The police and army are the protectors of apartheid."

"And you, and your property. Who did you phone when the house was burgled, the ANC or the police?"

"Can't you distinguish between petty criminals and freedom fighters?" Michael says, slamming his books down on the coffee table. "Besides, if there'd been an equitable distribution of wealth, there'd be less crime."

"More rhetoric. If such an idyllic situation should ever come to pass, you'll find it was easier to struggle for socialism than to live under it."

"Ignore him, Ma. He's trying to provoke me and today I won't provoke. He can't resist the throw-away line, the home-spun aphorism."

"Forget it," Paul says drily. "When'll lunch be ready?"

"It's ready, musteh," a large black woman says, wheeling in a server from the kitchen. "Hello Uncle Salmon. You don't come no more to the kitchen to see me, to say hello?"

"I was coming, Grace. You know I always come. I think you are the cleverest person in this house, the only one who doesn't talk nonsense about politics."

"Hau, the politics. They are killing each other in the township for the politics. We got no money for the rent, but they making the politics."

"If you've got no money for rent, Grace, that's politics," Michael says.

"You keep your white face out of the townships, Mikey, otherwise they will put an axe in your head. They don't ask about politics before they do that," Grace says, returning to the kitchen.

"Wise woman," Zalman says. "Not the breast, Lola. It tastes like wood, even when Grace makes it. I get splinters in the throat from it. You should taste the chicken at the Home."

"Grace will get into trouble one day," Michael says. "During the last consumer boycott she was caught by the comrades with a bagful of groceries she'd bought from Pick 'n Pay. She only got away with it because there was more of her than there was of them. She zonked one of them with the bottle of oil they threatened to make her drink. What a leader she'd make. Instead she's become a black middle-class yenta."

"Don't say such things. She brought you up. Can you believe it? She's been with us for seventeen years," Lola says. "How time has flown. And yet it seems like yesterday."

"She's our inheritance from the Singers," Paul tells Zalman. "The sister of their maid. You remember the Singers, don't you, Zalman? We used to be friendly with them in another life."

"What happened to them? Did they also emigrate? She was a nice young woman with red hair. I don't remember him so well."

"Not so young and not so red any more, is my guess. No, they didn't emigrate. They just moved on."

Lola flushes and is about to speak when Michael interrupts.

"I meant to tell you. Their daughter's moved in next door to us, she and two others. A letter came to us addressed to Sara Singer, so I took it in and introduced myself. I wouldn't have recognised her, haven't seen her since we were kids. She's tall, with long blond hair. Not a bad looker but a bit remote and not too friendly. Perhaps she's carrying on the family feud, or perhaps I'd interrupted her swotting. There was a skull and bones on her table, so she's either a witch-doctor or a medical student."

If Michael becomes friendly with Sara, Lola resolves, she will pack up and join Chantal in Sydney. It would be a relief to get away from everyone, from everything. Nobody needs her; not Paul, not Michael, not even Zalman. As for work, she isn't much good at it anyway. She feels even less effectual since she took over the correspondence. Those letters give her nightmares. At least she could apologise to the petitioners when she worked in the office. Now she cannot reply to the prisoners' letters without endangering them.

I read her like a book. Paul watches Lola flush and swallow her food, pushing down the cry which rises in her throat when Michael mentions Sara Singer. And she reads me like a book, a dirty book. One look and we stand revealed before one another, naked. Not much beauty between us. Me with my paunch and thin legs; she with her rolls and fat-dimpled thighs. Cellulose. Euphemism for fat. Once upon a time, with limbs entwined, we mated and begat three children, at well-spaced intervals, two kugels and a cactus plant. Not much of that any longer. Civilised: she in her bedroom, me in mine. Out of politeness, sometimes, not to make one another feel old, rejected. I dine out, occasionally, more from curiosity than passion. She's given up, I think. All that Reichian fuss about orgasm: stasis, neurosis, emotional plague. Cock and bull. Peaceful now, like the grave: she intuits the dry socket where my heart should be; and I the worm that eats into hers. Stuck together with the glue of inertia, habit. No point in parting now. Then, perhaps. Me and Ruth, she and Daniel; we'd have deserved one another. All that thunder and lightning, grief and betrayal. Remember the pain but not the love any more. Forgotten even what Ruth looks like: pale high forehead, red hair, green eyes. But how did they fit together? Gone. Forgotten. Fifteen years, twenty years, a hundred years. Great love. Great obsession more like it. Trick of nature to reproduce ourselves and to perpetuate the misery, the stupidity. And when we can't bear the emptiness, the meaninglessness, we make myths out of it. Yet I still drive past the house. Up the hill, along the narrow street, past the row of fir trees, see a light through the trees. Then the pipe dream: Come inside. Long time no see. All those wasted years. So pleased. Have a drink. Bring Lola over one day. Our ridge. How could she have built a house over the altar, the iron-age ruins, made rockeries out of stone-age tools? Best thing. Bury the past and place a tombstone over it, a nice, safe suburban house. Rest in peace. Times when I feel movement in that dry socket. Times when I don't know whom I miss more: him or her, friend or lover.

"Will you join us, Paul?" Lola's voice has a hard edge on it. "Tea or coffee?" She knows where he has been.

"Why do you always ask? You know I drink coffee."

"I suppose I keep hoping that you'll have a change of heart some day. And have tea." Lola's hand shakes a little as she pours the coffee into the cup.

Zalman looks out of the window; the pain is palpable. "I'm going into the garden," he says. "Since I started to make my own garden, I like to look at gardens. Little green things are starting to come up already. I am looking every day at the sky for rain. It is hard, schlepping that watering can from the tap. Good exercise, the occupational therapist tells me. Exercise. Therapy. In der'erd with the lot."

"Zalman, I wasn't going to mention it today but now that you have … The Director phoned me yesterday to say he'd like to speak to me. What have you been up to?"

"Me?" Zalman looks at her with wide eyes, his curved brows raised behind his glasses. "Nothing."

"He said it had something to do with the garden."

"It's that old fool Silverman, the slave-driver. If you want to study exploitation," Zalman turns to Michael, "you must go to his farms in the Eastern Transvaal. There was that big case once, in the papers. Slave labour. Prison labour. Terrible man, that. And now he's become a big macher in the Home. Gave them a lot of money and they built the Nachum Silverman Recreation Room. And he sits there every day like a big balebos, playing klabberjas and telling everyone how rich he is. His children don't even come to see him. Only one grandson comes, sometimes. To make sure he leaves him the money. A spy, that's what Nachum Silverman is. He sees me speaking often to Mr Sibiya who has got more sense in his little black finger than Silverman has in his whole head, so he makes up stories about me."

"Zalman, what kind of stories?"

"He said John Sibiya helped me make my garden. Him, a person who had three farms and three hundred slaves and never held a spade in his hands."

"Did he?"

"Did who? What?" Zalman sighs. "All right. In the beginning John Sibiya helped me move a little bit of soil. But I paid him and I was going to give him all the prize money, not only share it with him."

"Zalman, that's not the point. The idea was for the inma–, the people in the Home to make their own gardens."

"This inmate is not interested in digging in the garden. I like to sit in gardens, not make them. I have better things to do with my time, even if I can't think what at this moment."

"Why didn't you just say you didn't want to do it?"

"Because then they start taking your temperature and giving you enemas or sending you to second-childhood clinics. I just want to be left alone. I don't want to be, how do you call it, socialised. I want to be left alone."

Lola gets up and puts her arms around Zalman.

"I'm sorry, Zalman, I'm sorry. I know you're unhappy at the Home. Come and live with us. I should never have arranged..."

"Please. You are wetting my neck with your tears. Enough already. I am living where I am living. I am just not going to take their occupational therapy."

"Jesus, Ma, if you don't do it, I'll go to that bloody Director myself and tell him to get stuffed. Zalman, come and live with us. You don't belong with those old people. You're one of us, man."

"And what makes you think that's a compliment?' Zalman says. "Anyway, I haven't got a T-shirt. No message for the masses."

"I've got a shirt for you. God's a Goy, it says."

"Goyim exist."

Paul keeps quiet; this is Lola's house and Lola's family. Zalman is the last person he would like to have around all the time, but he feels safe; the old man's got too much pride. Wouldn't take a bean from Belle. Intelligent, well-read, an autodidact. Sharp. Feel he's looking right through you, even if he hasn't got insight into his own foibles. Worked like a devil at his tailoring all his life, and lost every penny he earned at poker.

Zalman feels tired suddenly. He needs to be alone, but there is no place he can go. He longs for his dingy room in Jeppe Street from which Lola 'rescued' him the previous year after he had come down with pneumonia. Scarcely big enough to hold a bed, a wardrobe, a table and chair, it had been home for fourteen years, a place to come to after he had shortened jeans and sewed in zips in Mr Patel's workshop. What Patel knew about tailoring he could put in his eye, the one with the cataract, and not go blind. But Patel never claimed to be a master craftsman, and he paid him well enough to save him from the charity of sister Bailka, alias Belle. He could come home, close the door, make himself a cup of tea, then lie down on his bed and read. The bathroom and toilet were down the passage, and he greeted the other four tenants who shared it with him without exchanging more than a dozen words a week. "You need care," Lola had said when she visited him in hospital. "You can't live like that any longer. You could collapse and lie there for days and nobody would know. I can't bear to think of it," she had said, weeping into a handkerchief. Weak from his illness and from the medicines they had pumped into him, he had surrendered his freedom and gone into the Home. He could not bear to cause Lola anxiety. She and Michael were the only people he really cared about.

"Michael, put out for me a chair under that big tree. I think I will sleep for a while," he says. "Enough fuss over Homes and gardens."

Later that afternoon, Lola takes him back to the Home. There is a queue of cars unloading the inmates.

"Just say the word, Zalman, and I'll come and fetch you and you'll live with us," Lola says as she kisses him goodbye.

"Enough already of that nonsense. If I left this place, they'd all die from boredom. I have a duty to perform. To keep them worried."

He watches her drive away. In all that beauty and luxury, among all those flowers and trees, there is much pain and unhappiness. And he can do nothing to lighten her burden. Like that old Yiddish song:

Die Blumen schmeken fein,
Es ken azei nisht zein,
Az chossen kala fielen schmerz un pein.

The sun is setting to the right of the hill. The clouds, swept by the wind into two great wings which hover over the ridge, are tinged with pink and red and orange. The grass, dry and brown, is ablaze with the dying light. Zalman wants to wrench his aching heart out of his chest and throw it to the ground.

Can there be no god when there is such beauty? Can there be a god when there is such pain?

EIGHT

Ezekiel Mzwakhe Sibiya hurries home from church before darkness and smog descend on the township. It is Sunday evening and in tomorrow's newspaper, which he will retrieve from the Director's wastepaper basket, he will read about the rape, murder, assault and robbery in the townships. Life is cheap here; for ten cents they will slit your throat. As he does not wish to become a statistic in the crime report, he bends his head against the dust which a sudden wind is blowing up, and, keeping to the middle of the road, potholed and strewn with garbage and goat droppings, he walks quickly towards his house. Those newspapers – he clucks his tongue angrily – they make us numbers, not people. Four people and one black killed in head-on collision, it said in Friday's paper. The names of the four 'people', whites, are given; the black one is nameless. If anyone misses a father, a husband, a son, let her queue outside the Mortuary at dawn and search for him there.

Names. Mr Sibiya often thinks about names. In the Bible – he reads the Bible diligently – it is written that Adam gave names to all the cattle and to the fowls and to the beasts.

"The white man makes games with names," he told Mr Zalman the other day. "He thinks he is Adam."

"Or even god," said Mr Zalman. "You know, Mr Sibiya, you are the only person I can speak to in this place. Tell me about your life."

"My life," he told Mr Zalman, "is too long. But I can tell about the names. First the white man called us Kaffir, then Native, then Bantu, then African. But only when we begin to call ourselves what we are, Black, did things begin to change. Names make magic. But you must know the right names."

The wind blows a piece of newspaper against Mr Sibiya's legs, interrupting the flow of his thoughts. Tomorrow, he decides, disentangling his legs from the paper, I will go to the Director and say: My name is Ezekiel Mzwakhe Sibiya. Ez... M...Maz... the Director will stutter; but why then do we call you John? Because the old Director said, Ez... Maz... it is too hard, we will call you John.

If I take back my right name, maybe things will go better, he thinks as he approaches home. Masilo will stop running with the comrades, Agnes will stop going with that policeman, and Mandla and Lindiwe will come back from Africa, Russia, I do not know where they are. Four years now since they ran away, just after Soweto. Soweto this, Soweto that. Why do people always say Soweto? Is that the only place where the black people live and suffer? What about Alexandra, Guguletu, Katlehong, Tembisa and all the others?

"The Government," he told Mr Zalman, "always says, go back home. All right, I answer, I will go back home. And where is home? Where I was born. And where was I born? Alexandra township. I was born there two years after the 'flu epidemic and two years before the Big Mine Strike. 1920, it is written in my pass."

"I am seventeen years older than you," Mr Zalman had said. "But go on, tell me more."

"I have seen the place where my father was born, on the farm of Fanie du Plessis, in the Northern Transvaal, but I have never seen the place where my grandfathers were born, before the Voortrekkers came with their guns and took away our land. My father worked many years for Fanie du Plessis and had

62

some cattle and had some land. Your cattle are getting too fat, Fanie says to my father. They are eating all my grass. You must leave this place. So my father must sell his cattle and leave the land where he was born. When he comes to Alexandra township in the year before the first Big War, he can still buy a little land, freehold, so we had one cow, and two goats and some chickens in the backyard. With his horse and cart he takes the people to the city because there is no train and no bus. My mother and her sisters did build our house with mud bricks, and the children did play in the veld, near the Jukskei river, which is the same river that is down there in the valley, opposite the Home. And we learn to read and to write in the church hall. That time there was no school in the township."

"I have never heard such a story before," said Mr Zalman. "Please tell me more, Mr Sibiya."

"Then the locusts come. Big black clouds hiding the sun, like it says in the Bible, and they finish off everything on the farms. And there is no rain, and the people got nothing to eat. So they come like the locusts to Alex. In that time you must not have the pass to live in Alex so many many people can come. In the backyards they make the shacks from corrugated iron and coal sacks and boxes, and make the beer and gamble and kill each other. Then the white people begin to shout, we need more land, move the natives, break down the houses, build the hostels for our workers. So they begin to move us to Meadowlands and to Diepkloof in South Western Townships, which is the right name for Soweto. I will not go, I tell my brothers. Our father bought this land, freehold, and our mother and her sisters built this house. In Soweto they will give me a shoe box and charge me the rent. We don't want trouble, say my brothers, and they go to Meadowlands. There is trouble, but I stay. I've got the job in the Home and Maria got washing in the new white houses, and the children go to school. Now it is not like before. There is the schools, there is a clinic, there is buses and taxis. There is also too many people and too much fighting and trouble, but what can you do? This is our place. We can work, we can eat, and we got Section 10. If you don't get Section 10, you must go home. And where is home? And where is the work? The Government doesn't worry about that. They just send the police to arrest you for your pass."

"Mr Sibiya," Mr Zalman said. "You have had a very hard life. Tell me what this Section 10 is."

"Pass, kaffir! Pass, kaffir! the police are shouting when you are sleeping with your wife in the backyard of the house where she is working. Even you got the pass, they say that word: tres-pass, and you pay the fine. If you not got the pass, they send you to the jail, to the prison farm, to the homeland, and the life is very hard. Tres-pass. You haven't got the pass, you tres-pass. My English is not good. You can hear how I am speaking. It is only when I am speaking my home language, I can say properly what I am thinking. Yes, Mr Zalman, I can read the newspaper and the Bible but Agnes must explain to me what is tres-pass. I think, Mr Zalman, I can speak the Yiddish better than the English. I am working thirty years in the Home, and the old people speak only a little bit English, so I learn the Yiddish from them. Maybe it is easy because I know a little bit Afrikaans."

"You learned Yiddish," Mr Zalman said, "because you are clever. You are much cleverer than Mr Silverman, for example, who is a person that is so stupid and so evil, that he can only make trouble. Like he made for us when you helped me dig the garden."

"Yes, Mr Zalman. Mr Silverman is talking all the time about the chazershe schwartze or schwartze ganovim, the black pigs and the black thieves. Because he is in the Home only a little time, he does not know that the chazershe schwartzer, John Sibiya, understands the Yiddish."

"What a pity, Mr Sibiya, that you cannot read Yiddish. If you could, I would let you read what I write in my little black note book. You would understand better than most people what I am writing about. You must tell me more about your life some other time. I can see the Chinaman is here and you want to go to play Fah Fee. You must tell me, one day, what the game Fah Fee is. I am starting to be interested why all the black people who work in the Home get together at two o'clock in the afternoon and again at eight o'clock in the evening, and stand there, near the trees at the side of the Home, and wait for the Chinaman. I know the game has to do with dreams and with a lottery. I am very interested in dreams and even more interested in lotteries. I used to be a gambler when I was young. So I am beginning to get an idea."

Mr Sibiya hopes it is a better idea than the one Mr Zalman had about the gardening. That nearly made trouble for him with the Director. But because he has been at the Home for thirty years and because he does his job nicely, the Director does not make trouble for him. He just says, John, you must help these old people, but sometimes they do not understand what they are doing, so you must be careful. Mr Sibiya thinks that Mr Zalman knows very well what he is doing, but he has decided that if he wants to keep out of trouble, he must be very careful about Mr Zalman's ideas.

There is smoke coming from Mr Sibiya's chimney and he knows that Maria is cooking supper for him.

"Maria is a good woman," he told Mr Zalman who has never been married. "It was right to marry someone from the farms. The town women just want the money and the clothes. Maria just wants the children, seven children like her mother had. Why? I am asking her. To starve? To go to jail? To be killed? We haven't got enough trouble with four children? To look after us when we are old, Maria says. Seven children must look after two people when they are old? I say to Maria. We must do like the white people do: when you are sick or old or mad, you must send them to the Home. Maria is always cross when I am saying that. What will our Ancestors say if we do that thing? she is asking me. They did not live in the Home. She wants it to be like in the old days, on the farms."

"The old days," Mr Zalman had said. "Ah yes, the old days."

Before Mr Sibiya goes into his house he looks around at his neighbourhood. In the old days it was different. Four hundred houses have already been demolished and his friends and relatives have been moved to Diepkloof, Meadowlands and

Tembisa. His house and those of a few neighbours are still standing, like rotten teeth in an old man's mouth, with big gaps between them. I will not move out, he used to say to Maria. They will have to pull down the house with me inside. Then last year the Reverend made that Save Alex Committee and they stopped pulling down houses. Now they are talking about reverse policy, a garden city, new houses, new roads, electricity. But the people are worried. In the beginning they trusted the Reverend and his Committee, but now they are saying that he has made an arrangement with the Government: the people without Section 10 will have to go, freehold will be replaced by leasehold, the old houses will be knocked down and only the people with money will get loans to build new houses. The poor people and the people without Section 10, will be sent to the homelands, to starve.

"Garden suburb!" Welcome Mphlope had shouted out at the meeting. "Yes! You cannot make the garden without manure, and we got plenty manure in the street and in the Committee."

Everybody laughed because they knew that only a drunk man like Welcome would say a thing like that. But there is talk of bribes, extortion, corruption. The Reverend, they say, is building a shop on the other side of the Jukskei; the Committee has still got freehold and rent is going up. If you can't afford to pay rent for a house, the Reverend said at the last meeting, move to a room. So the people are not happy. Especially the young people.

Mr Sibiya looks up at the sky. The sun is sinking behind golden clouds that stretch across the sky like the wings of an angel. God is in Heaven, all's right with the world, he says out of habit. But he knows all is not right, and he wonders how much is God's fault, and how much the people's fault.

It is warm and pleasant inside the house. The stove, the ice box and the kitchen dresser are in a small alcove overlooking the backyard, and the table and chairs, on which Mr Sibiya still owes money to a hire-purchase company, stand at the centre of the living room. Maria bought the sofa and two armchairs from

Mrs Mason whose 'ironing girl' she has been for the past eight years. He and Maria have one bedroom, the children share, or used to share, the other room. They do not have electricity, and the toilet and shower are in the backyard. For this, Maria said when he refused to move out, you will let them kill you with the bulldozer? Your brothers were clever; they moved out. They must do what they must do, but I am not moving from my father's house, he had told her.

Maria is stirring a pot of mealie meal on the stove, Agnes is sitting on the sofa, painting her nails, and even Masilo is home tonight, reading the newspaper. Masilo starts to argue with him even before he has taken off his hat and jacket and put on his old cardigan.

"So," he says, "what did the parents say about the school boycott?"

"I went to church," Mr Sibiya answers.

"Yes, but afterwards. We know all about it. You are trying to get us back to school and we won't go. We are sick of gutter education."

"A gutter education is better than no education," Agnes says, blowing on her blood-red finger nails. "We've got to fight them with their own weapons."

"What weapons did you get with your matric? Nails and a paint brush?" Masilo asks angrily.

He turns back to his father. "You fought the government in the Save Alex Campaign, but when it comes to schooling, you won't support us."

"If you don't go to school, you will sweep floors like me."

"If I go to school, I'll be beaten by the ignorant teachers, and tear-gassed by the police. They're there every day, the police, making sure we swallow the poison the system feeds us. You know how corrupt everything is. Remember how ashamed you were when we were sent home from school because you couldn't afford to buy the new uniform, and how angry you were when we found out later that our headmaster was getting bribes from a clothing manufacturer to change the uniform every few years?"

"The government will not speak to us until you are back at school. Do that thing and we will help you."

"You can't work with the System," Masilo says bitterly, "You have to fight it. They promise and do nothing. Go back to school, they said after 1976, we will fix things. They didn't even fix our roof, forget about the other things."

"Why should they?" Agnes says, "you burned it down."

"You were also in the 1976 uprising, but you have changed, Agnes, and everybody has noticed it."

"Shut up! It's not true! I just don't want any more trouble in the family. Look at our mother and father. They have grown old since Lindiwe and Mandla went away. We don't even know where they are. Isn't that enough trouble?"

"It is enough!" Mr Sibiya says sternly. "Can't we sit down and eat in peace like other families? Yes, we did have a meeting after church. Even the Committee agrees that the boycott must stop. You must get the education, even if it is not such a good one."

"They teach us rubbish," Masilo says. "They teach us about the brave Afrikaners who left the Cape to get freedom from the English, but they don't teach us about the brave black people who fought against the Voortrekkers for their own freedom. They teach us about Shakespeare, but we don't know the praise poems of our own people. They teach us to be servants and workers and they teach the white students to be masters and managers. We want equal education, not slave education. and you don't understand because you are happy to eat the crumbs your white bosses at the Home throw you."

"Leave him alone." Agnes stops painting her nails. "You got your education and your clothes and your food from those crumbs."

"Don't you see what they're doing? They're using education to get control of our minds, to make us into hewers of wood and drawers of water, like it says in your Bible," Masilo turns to his father.

"Let us eat now," Maria says, spooning the mealie meal onto the plates and topping it with stewed meat. "It is enough fighting. If the family is fighting, what can happen to the nation?"

"You disappear for days, then you turn up suddenly, making trouble," Agnes says.

"I'm sick of all this!" Masilo shouts. He picks up the paper and goes to the door. "And you, Agnes, had better look out. Nobody trusts you any more. One day you and that shit policeman will be in trouble, I'm warning you!"

Agnes leaps up with a shout and lunges at Masilo. He grabs her wrists, pushes her on to the sofa, then goes out of the room, slamming the door behind him.

"Now look what you've done!" Maria shouts at Agnes. "He hasn't been home for days. I don't know what he eats or where he sleeps. But I know where you are sleeping, and don't think you can bring me a baby to look after. I will throw you out, together with the baby. Ai, ai, what I have done that the Ancestors should punish me with such terrible children?"

Mr Sibiya bends his head over the plate and spoons the food into his mouth, slowly, without appetite, like the old people do in the Home, cutting himself off from the angry words that are flying over his head. Tomorrow, he decides, he will go to the Director and say, my name is Ezekiel Mzwakhe Sibiya. If the Director says, it is easier to call you John, he will get very angry and answer: Perhaps it is easier to say John than Ezekiel Mzwakhe Sibiya, but that is my name and that is what I want to be called.

It is time that everything should be called by the right name.

NINE

8 May 1980

... You're right, Jeanne. These days I'm the one who's apologising for not writing regularly. With the help of Mary, who's been working at the Advice Office for years, I've overcome my blocks and reservations, and am more active than ever. I really feel I'm doing something meaningful, for the first time. We've been going out to the black townships to meet with mothers whose children have been detained for boycotting the schools. We're trying to organise a joint protest. You can't imagine the atmosphere in the townships these days. One has the feeling of standing over a volcano which is about to erupt. Only chaos and destruction can result from such ominous rumblings.

Yes, I'm still doing the correspondence, though it's only a part of my activities now. I'm pleased you're so interested in those excerpts I've been sending you. I agree: the real voice of the people comes through in those letters. There's so much rhetoric flying around these days, especially in that so-called literary journal, *Skelm,* which made its appearance several months ago. A great fuss is being made of it, the voice of the

71

people and that sort of thing, but I find it boring, unreadable. It is pretentious in an inverted kind of way. I'm not surprised. I know some of the people who work on it...

No bother; I'll send you copies of the letters from time to time. I can understand that you feel angry, frustrated and helpless when you read them, but at least you want to know what's going on in this country. I suppose people react in different ways. I sent a few excerpts to Chantal as well. She replied that she's trying to forget the misery she left behind. That's another way of coping, I suppose ... More excerpts follow.

Dear Sir,
I hereby wish to enquire about the business of Section 10 (a) qualification as to where and how they really works to a person of my nature.

First and famous my parent i.e. my mother, was born in Klerksdorp farms then she moved to Fochville where I was borne and bread. What steps should I take in this hard life? ... I mean, having a matric certificate and being jobless is tantamount to being a poor rack without a head...

(No hope for getting Section 10 rights: His mother was born in the rural areas and he won't get permission to work in town, where the jobs are.)

Dear Sir and Madam,
I have a problem wich worry me every day. If you can help me please try. My problem is about qualifications of staying in the location. I want to stay in prescribed areas becuase of too many reason, if required I will gladly supply...

Sir,
I here by writing this letter to you. Please advis me as you advis many people. I have done the affidavit at the Commissioner of Oaths. I have been at the office five times. They are telling me such stories which I don't understand. And they don't even use these affidavit. They said they don't believe it. And now all this stories makes me sad. Could you please HELP?

Dear Sir,
I'm very sorry to make these few lines to you but I cant help
because I'm looking for someone to help me...

Madam,
I am working for a firm here in Boksburg. I think I am now
four months hurt in this firm and I have been attended at a
hospital here, Natalspruit hospital, with a fracture leg because
we are working with dangerous articles. Infect, these are mine
steel articles.
    Up to now I didn't even hear a mention about compensation
of this fractured leg. All I am expected to do is just to work
sincerely with that disabled swollen leg. Madam, what must I
do, really? Sir,

Kindly Sir,
Will you please sir help me. I am living very sadness. I have no
home, no pass. I am still owing the law an old tax ... Yours
orbident

To whom it may be concerned
I have decided to write to you since I am in a tarable condition
plus the situation of injustice and oppression...

Sir,
I am too far from my family and I don't get any visit becuase
of lacking money. My father packed away and leave this
world and my mother pays rent, school fees, food, water and
many more. So please have mercy for me, being a parent
yourself. Sir please help me as you have helped others like me.
Yours obedient

The president,
I am writing this letter with tears rolling down my cheeks.
Sir I'm a prisoner serving nine (9) years for housebreaking and
theft.

I'm now five (5) years in prison. Sir, my complain is about my parole, becuase the half of the sentence is over ... Yours obedient

Kindly Sir,
I, the above prisoner write in request for you to give help on my behalf. I'm a convict serving a period of six years imprisonment for robbery ... I was told to serve half my sentence but to my dispondment I am still already in custody. I am been hit by difficulties hepening at my family and my father is of age 73 years old. I have lost my late mother May last year. My sister December and my younger brother who was a breadwinner during my absence died May this year.

So I request your hand in this matter. I ask you to apply an application on release for me or of parole for confirmation write or send your agents at home because my father really don't know what to do to put things wright at home. I hope my request will be considered with father dedication. Thanking you in anticipation.

Yours obedient

...I'll try to write more regularly, Jeanne. It's just that there's so much work to get through. I take the correspondence home and do it at night. Love, Ma.

TEN

It is a hot Saturday morning in November. Sara returned from the market a short while ago and is sitting at the kitchen table, adding up columns of figures that yield a different total each time she checks them. On the floor lie heaps of plums, peaches and mangoes. Pockets of onions and potatoes sag against tomato boxes, and under the table, next to her feet, is a carton of wilting lettuce, flanked by cabbages and cauliflower.

She glances from the mess on the floor to the mess in her notebook. A vegetable co-op had sounded like a good idea when she moved to Crown Mines last year. Now it has become a dreaded chore. Every six weeks she takes orders from five households, drives down Main Reef Road to the market, pushes a trolley through great halls stacked with boxes, sacks and crates, then lifts, stacks and carries her purchases from floor to trolley, hall to car and car to kitchen, where she sorts the orders and calculates what each household owes her. She had visualised a leisurely stroll among stalls of aromatic fruit and vegetables, attended by friendly, rosy-cheeked farmers, the sort one sees in travel brochures. Instead she has to deal with loud-mouthed vendors who shout obscenities across the echoing halls or whisper tips to aficionados for that afternoon's race meeting. Selling vegetables to small buyers like herself is an affliction they suffer with bad grace.

She is expected at her parents' home for lunch, but her prospects of getting there before one o'clock grow dimmer as the figures become less and less intelligible. Sara gets up, pins her hair into a top-knot, changes from jeans and a T-shirt into a light summer dress, then settles down once again to disentangle lists of fruit and vegetables from prices, people and quantities.

She would gladly switch to the greengrocer up the road, but at this stage the co-op is her only real link with the community. She enjoys living in her tiny house with its wooden strip flooring and pressed-iron ceilings, the patch of garden with its picket fence, and the corrugated iron roof on which the rain drums loudly in summer. She likes the mine dumps, the untarred streets and the eucalyptus plantation at the edge of the village. If she climbs to the top of the mine dump near her house, the city, with its cheese-grater buildings, appears to float above it, to be in touching distance.

The few working-class families who have remained in the village have little to do with the students to whom they refer as 'kommuniste'. The compounds of the black miners, several kilometres up the road, are empty, the miners having returned to Maputo, Malawi and other front-line states: Local blacks have always been reluctant to work in the mines. Sara has climbed through a hole in the surrounding wall and walked through the deserted compound. The concrete bunks, long rows of unwalled toilets, cold-water showers, barbed wire fences and the high security lights which surround the compound have left indelible images, calling to mind photographs she has seen of concentration camps. She averts her eyes every time she drives past the compound.

Laura and Marlene moved out of the house after a few months, Laura to a flat in Yeoville – they're not my kind of people, she had said of the neighbours – and Marlene to Rhodes University where she is studying Drama. Sara has known them since high school, though they were never close friends. Marlene had played lead roles in school dramas, and Laura had been head girl. Neither has quite recovered from the glory of her school days: Marlene has retained her theatrical voice and gestures; and Laura's organisational gift, for lack of a nobler outlet, had expressed itself in near-tyrannical household management. She would have winced at the mess in the kitchen and sneered at the botched-up sums. Sara smiles; she enjoys living alone.

Come home, her mother has pleaded, it's unsafe in that house; it isn't even burglar-proofed. But Sara feels she is living in a forgotten corner of the city, scorned by burglars as an area of poor pickings. So safe does she feel here, that she often forgets to lock the front door when she leaves for Medical School in the morning.

Although she is naturally outgoing, she has not made close friends among her neighbours: She does not belong to a political organisation, hence cannot be assessed and labelled. To say "I'm not a joiner" would draw greater contempt; the uncommitted are scorned. A thaw has recently set in. When Gillian, a member of the vegetable co-op, heard that Sara had worked in a rural clinic during her December vacation, she invited her to speak in a study group in the village. Sara spent weeks researching infant mortality among blacks and relating it to her experience in the clinic. She had given the talk the previous evening and might have redeemed herself in the eyes of her neighbours. She does not consciously woo her neighbours' good opinion, but would find it more pleasant to be accepted as a member of the community.

The only neighbour who has shown real interest in her is Michael Stern, who at that very moment is vaulting over the low wall which separates their houses. He is wearing black running shorts and a yellow T-shirt. MAKE WAR ON EXPLOITERS, it demands, NOT LOVE TO SWEETHEART UNIONS. His political affiliations are spelled out on his T-shirts, and being a man of many interests, he has a large collection of shirts. He is a final year Arts student majoring in Industrial Sociology, who is also active in the incipient black trade union movement. She hears him play his

77

guitar late into the night and has seen his cartoons in student magazines and in End Conscription Campaign publications. She feels she has known him all her life, which, in a manner of speaking, she has, if you don't count the years between the ages of five and twenty. Since she moved in he has besieged her for loans of sugar, eggs and milk – none of which he ever returns – and with invitations to come and see his etchings. He is aware of her reluctance to become friends, and delights in provoking her into rejecting his half-serious invitations. She is puzzled by the unease she feels in his presence; she is usually relaxed with men. She grew up in the company of her brother and his friends; most of the students in her class are male; she has had several love affairs from which she has emerged relatively unscathed. Why, then, does she keep her distance from Michael? It might be some atavistic form of tribal loyalty. Not that he isn't insufferable in his own right. She turns back to her figures. Michael Stern is the last person she wishes to see right now.

"Such abundance!" he says, making his way over the piles of fruit. "Yet people say there is hunger in the land."

"Stop acting. Your share," Sara says without looking up, "is next to the kitchen dresser. And if you feel too guilty to eat it, donate it to Operation Hunger."

"I'm not acting, just dramatising, for the benefit of the uninitiated, the ironic fact that South Africa produces enough food to meet 110 per cent of the optimum daily energy requirements of the whole population, yet..."

"Uninitiated indeed! Those are my figures you're quoting!"

"I thought that might get your attention. Let me finish. Yet black children are dying from kwashiorkor, marasmus and pellagra, the result of a protein deficiency which leads to the swelling of limbs, a wasting away, mental derangement and death. Nearly a third of all African babies born in Grahamstown last year, for example, died of malnutrition before they were one year old."

"You have a retentive memory."

"You did well last night." Michael packs his vegetables into one of the empty boxes that stands near the stove. "Your audience was suitably impressed. There they were, all these months, thinking you were just another pretty face, a kugel like your ex-housemates, only to discover that you spend all your free time at rural clinics curing TB, measles and gastroenteritis, a veritable Albertina Schweitzer..."

"I made no such claims! I was merely giving my own impressions together with some facts I read up about health conditions in the rural areas."

"And drawing the wrong conclusions."

Sara wishes he would go away. He takes up all the air and space in a room. A deluded person might draw the wrong conclusion from such a physical reaction, but she knows she is not in the least attracted to him. She simply does not know how to handle a person who thinks he is God's gift to women. The stream of females that pours into the house he shares with Keith and Joe – both of whom have steady girlfriends – do not go there for the political enlightenment he dispenses so liberally. Not, that is, if one is to judge from the ecstatic look on their faces as they ride pillion on his motor cycle. She can see, of course, why they find him so attractive. He is tall, an ectomorph with a typically lean, long-limbed body, has dark, unruly hair and thick slanted eyebrows over deepset brown eyes. His nose is heavy, but he has such a warm, beguiling smile, that one's eyes somehow skip over it. All this charm, however, leaves her stone-cold.

"We don't need bigger or better hospitals," he is saying as he bites into an unwashed peach. "We need a restructuring of our whole society. The diseases you described are caused by sickness in the social fabric, not merely by viruses and bacteria. You medics cure the symptoms, then send the people back into the very conditions that create these diseases."

"Health workers do what they're trained to do, cure people, not societies," she says.

"And then they sit back and wait for them to return, re-infected. You've got to get to the root of the problem..."

"You're a pain in the neck, Michael Stern. Please take your fruit and go."

Michael laughs. "I suspect I'm not welcome. How much do I owe you?"

"It's a gift," she says wearily, pushing aside her pen and notebook.

"You mean you can't work it out?" He looks down at her scruffy calculations. "Okay, I'll help you. I am highly gifted. I can add, subtract, multiply and divide." Sara is about to say, I can manage on my own, but she has reached a point of such desperation, that rather than become the laughing stock of the vegetable co-op, she is prepared to accept Michael's offer.

"Thanks," she mumbles.

"I can't work with my feet in the cabbages. Let's go into the lounge."

The 'lounge' is a small room that leads off the kitchen, with a table, three chairs, a tattered sofa and two armchairs. Michael sinks onto the two-seater sofa and pats the place next to him.

"Sit here. I need explanations. Yesus, what confusion. You must be totally innumerate."

She bites back an angry response, and as she sits down, the cushion subsides towards the centre, tilting her towards him.

"Nice," he says without looking up from the lists he is compiling on a new page. "Stay where you are, and I'll give you a dazzling display from simple arithmetic to calculus."

Her first reaction is to move away, but that is what Michael would expect. She decides to call his bluff, to beat him at his own game. He is an incorrigible flirt who needs to be taught a lesson. It might then become possible to be friends without sparks flying between them. She leans even further towards him and a stray lock of her hair brushes his face. Startled, he turns towards her, but when their eyes meet, she draws back. What keeps her sitting is the sudden flush that floods his face and the intense yet puzzled look with which he holds her eyes. She seems to lose awareness of time or place, until she hears him draw a deep breath and say, "These scribbles, I assume, mean that Gillian, Dawn and Kevin each want a third of a bag of potatoes, and half a box of tomatoes..."

He is very quiet as he writes down her instructions, sorting out each person's order, working out quantities, calculating how much each household owes her. Occasionally her knee, through the thin fabric of her dress, touches his, and she draws away. Once, his arm brushes against hers and he apologises, turning back abruptly to his calculations. It is very quiet in the house. Outside, the cicadas burst into fitful shrillness, leaving an even greater silence as their song subsides. The chugging of a train in the distance is an accompaniment to the beating of her heart. Sara wants to break the enfolding silence with music, but her body seems fused into the sofa, and she is unable to get to the turntable.

"That's it," he says, putting the notebook down on the floor. Then he turns to her and takes her face between his hands. Drawing her gently towards him, he kisses her eyes, her cheeks, her mouth, with increasing ardour. She puts her arms around him, and somehow it no longer matters who is teaching whom a lesson.

"Lost time," he murmurs as he loosens her hair and buries his face in her neck. "Wanted to do this from the moment I saw your skull and bones."

"My what?" She draws away, laughing.

"After you moved in, I stole the mail out of your letter box and pretended it had been delivered to me. And there were all those bones on the table, and a skull resting on *Gray's Anatomy*. And you, the ice maiden, bearing grudges about skeletons in our respective family cupboards..."

"Oh God!" She sits up straight. "My mother should see me now."

"And mine?" Michael pulls her towards him and kisses her. As they draw apart, he says, "If she saw us now, she'd slap a life-time ban on any further intimacies."

There is a loud knocking on the front door; the members of the co-op have come to claim their vegetables.

Everyone seems to sense that this is not the time to discuss infant mortality with Sara, but they do say, interesting talk, we must discuss it sometime, horrifying figures, and other phrases that hold a promise of future communication. They take their purchases, pay her and leave. She phones her mother and cancels the lunch arrangement.

"And it isn't because you studied T. S. Eliot when I was young, or became a writer when you should have been taking me to the circus. I have a lot of sorting out to do just now," she says, "so I'll come for lunch tomorrow. You're going to a poetry reading in Soweto? Okay, I'll come for supper on Monday."

"I almost never lie to her," she tells Michael who is lying on the sofa with his legs dangling over the arm rest, "but if she knew I was going out with you on your motorcycle, she'd think she'd failed as a mother."

"My mother would burst all her lachrymal glands. Et tu, Brute, you brute! she would cry, sinking to the ground in a pool of tears. Not enough that her husband has been in love with your mother all his life; now her son..."

"My mother, your father, WHAT?"

"You didn't know? When they were young, in that Movement of theirs, long before my mother came on the scene. But that doesn't seem to matter; she feels your mother was there before her and that she somehow imprinted herself on wherever it is that one imprints, and that my father has not been able to love anyone since. But that's not all..."

"Wait. Let that sink in. My mother and your father were, uh, involved before they were married to my father and your mother?"

"Worse. While we were young and helpless, our parents were apparently – and I say apparently advisedly – great friends who partied and holidayed together. Then – wait for it – your father and my mother fell in love. Call it revenge, call it just desserts, but that's what happened."

"Michael Stern, take your vegetables and go home. You're making all this up."

"I forgive your incredulity, especially as you're apparently hearing it for the first time. I may be telling this in a light-hearted manner, but believe me, it's a saga of love, disloyalty, betrayal, regret, the lot. We've got to do better. We'll make up for it, heal their wounds, bring together the Montagues and Capulets, stop the bloodletting. Did you really not know?"

Sara shakes her head. "I knew there was something between our families but my mother always evaded the subject. She said she'd tell me when I was older. I've just aged ten years."

"In our family everything hangs out. You feel something, you say it. A bloody battlefield. The only time my parents aren't attacking one another is when they combine forces to demolish someone else. A couple who hates together, remains together."

"In our family, everything is so controlled, so civilised. Not in front of the children. I sense a deep sadness in my mother, a withdrawal in my father, a few disconnected wires, yet the façade remains unshattered. Who are they protecting anyhow?" Sara is surprised by the bitterness she feels.

"Don't grieve." Michael takes her into his arms and holds her close. "I think I love you."

"Don't say such things! We don't even know one another. Just an hour ago you were the last person I wanted to see..."

"And now?"

"There's an undeniable attraction."

"That'll do for a start. Come. I know a little wooded place with a small waterfall nearby. It's a beautiful day, we're young, free, and life is wonderful, worth fighting for. Let's take a break from revolution and gastroenteritis and starvation and delinquent parents for an hour or two. Have you ever been on a motor cycle?"

"No. But judging from the look on your lady-friends' faces, it must be a fantastic experience."

"Ah! I detect a note of you-know-what. Anyway, those are Comrades, not lovers. Believe me."

"I don't. But I'm not into jealous scenes. I'm my own person and you are yours. Loz leben, laat lewe, let live. My motto."

"My very own credo. You couldn't have expressed it more succinctly."

She goes into her bedroom and changes back into her jeans and shirt. He takes his vegetables and fruit home, and re-emerges carrying two helmets, one of which he gives her.

"Don't you lock your door?" Michael asks as they leave the house.

"I haven't anything worth stealing. You don't have burglaries here, do you?"

"Plenty. Sometimes just food gets stolen. But I make sure my camera is locked away, out of sight. And I suggest you do the same with anything of saleable value. We live in a deprived society..."

"No lectures. Just boy and girl going out for a joy ride. We may never feel so, well you know, again." She cannot bring herself to say 'happy'; everything is moving too fast. She can only contain this overwhelming feeling if she keeps up a bantering tone. She suspects Michael feels the same.

She does not feel happy for long. That was not ecstacy she had seen on those women's faces; that was terror. Sara twines her arms tightly around Michael's waist as he turns the corner at a forty-five degree angle, and roars over the bumpy sand road, up a narrow tarred street, under a railway bridge, towards the Main Reef Road, where they come to a stop at a traffic light.

"Remember the Struggle!" she says breathlessly. "Don't throw away your life on a fast ride. You still have work to do. And even if you haven't, I have. Let live!"

He laughs, turns around and kisses her. "You'll live. Hold tight," he says, "and on love's light wheels I'll transport you to a little paradise on the West Rand where we'll exchange love's eternal vows."

"*Romeo and Juliet* was our set work as well," she says. "Don't get carried away. We live in very prosaic times."

"Wrong. We live in the most extraordinary time. Anything can happen, and it usually does. Look what's happening to us."

He looks left and right, then slips into the main street, against a bright red traffic light. Sara tightens her hold around Michael's waist and rests her head against his back. Not since Selina carried her around on her back as a child, has she felt so close to anyone.

ELEVEN

The interview takes an unexpected turn. Nicholas is forced onto the defensive and Mogorosi is goaded into an extreme black power stand. Ruth, in the office next door, imagines Simon Sibandla's triumph as he leans back in his chair, arms across belly, chins and fat-folds of neck quivering over his caftan collar. He has manoeuvred a 'colonialist' – one with great influence among young black writers – into agreeing that the white writer has no role in post-apartheid society, and a Black Consciousness man into making statements that will undermine their fragile working relationship. The headlines, in the newspaper for which Simon works, will soon proclaim: 'White Literature Empty, Lacks Black Experience; Black writers Aim at Liberation.'

"...an explosion of black writing," Nicholas is saying to Simon, "a new wave ... nothing like it since the writing renaissance of the fifties, before the government snuffed it out by gagging black writers or forcing them into exile."

"Don't tell me history," Simon growls, "I was part of it while you were still playing on the fields of Eton."

"Well, hardly," Nicholas protests mildly. "King Edwards isn't exactly Eton."

"All the same," Simon mumbles, "elitist education."

Ruth despairs at Nicholas' naivety. Does he expect congratulations from Simon for being midwife to a cultural revolution?

"As a white man you have no right to act as spokesman for black writers, even if you are publishing *Skelm*," Simon says.

"I was invited by the organisers of the conference to speak on censorship," Nicholas says quietly, "because, as a publisher, I have first-hand knowledge of how censorship affects black writers in this country, not because I claim to be a spokesman for black writers."

"But some white writers try to voice the aspirations of the black community." Simon retreats a little, rattling off half a dozen names. "What can they know about the black man's experience, his suffering?"

"Nothing," Mogorosi answers the question put to Nicholas. "For them it's an academic exercise. Their writing may be good technically, but it's empty of all emotion. They don't understand the true feelings of the people. They know only the life of the privileged. They try to imagine the Black Experience but for us literature is life, we live it. We do not write for fame and glory or fortune. Our commitment is to truth, which is total liberation."

"Well, Nicholas?" It is Nicholas' head Simon wants.

"Look, I've said it before: white writers cannot and do not really know or feel the black man's life of suffering from the inside. I sometimes think that the most productive course for white writing would be to base imaginative work on the study of history, alternative history ..."

Ruth sighs. Simon has his head on the platter.

"History!" Simon explodes. "What history? Whose history? Alternative history? We're mainstream, man, not alternative..."

Nicholas placates him. It used to exasperate Ruth when Nicholas played down his role in the black writing renaissance. Since she has read *The Wretched of the Earth*, she at least understands the reasons.

"You've never read Fanon?" Nicholas had asked, incredulous. "We had other prophets," she replied. The following day he had brought her a well-thumbed copy of the book. "I still don't think all so-called colonialists would be irrelevant in new society," she had said after she read it, "and I don't believe that violent change is inevitable." "You don't understand," – he often prefaces his discussions with this phrase – "Decolonised people reject the humanism of the West as an ideology of lies, as a justification for pillage. And don't forget, you and I, like the rest of the whites, are the beneficiaries of that pillage; we have no right to colonise their struggle as well." "I do understand," Ruth had insisted, "but I refuse to stand on the sidelines and cheer on my own destruction. Not if I'm to continue living here." "Decolonisation is destructive, and violent. The colonised have this deep need to burn away the rot, together with the memory of their humiliation." He obviously knew the book by heart.

Ruth can neither slough off her abhorrence of violence, nor her need to be part of the process of change. She would like to say: "Mea culpa, chatiti, I have sinned, forgive me my trespasses, and accept my contribution to the new order." "You want to join us?" the blacks could, with justice, reply. "Move into Soweto, Alexandra, or any other black slum of your choice and give up your privileges." At this point she feels the full force of her ambivalence.

In the meantime, she accepts her limited role, and despite herself, has been swept along by the excitement generated by *Skelm* and its writers. In the beginning she had worked three afternoons a week. Now she is working a full day, five days a week, and takes manuscripts home to read. The print run of *Skelm* magazine has leapt from one thousand to seven thousand, and it has also spawned Skelm Publications. In the ten months Ruth has been working in the office, they have brought out four books, two by black writers, one by a 'coloured' poet and a novel by a white writer.

Much of the excitement is generated by uncertainty: will Skelm become a unique South African publishing house, or will it go broke? The chances of its being obliterated by bannings and censorship are great. Nicholas has written to the Publications Control Board saying that poems, stories and plays are not arms caches, and that black writers are not terrorists: they are writing about the frustrations and hopes of a voiceless people to which it might be wise to listen. But the censors are punitive, not wise.

Ruth does not doubt Nicholas' sincerity: He really believes that white 'colonialist' intellectuals are expendable and that after he has made his contribution, he will hand over Skelm Publications to Mogorosi, Thami and the others. But she sees very clearly the tangle of contradictions in which he is ensnared. He is widely regarded as the wunderkind of South African publishing. He has been interviewed by local and overseas newspapers and has spoken on public platforms about censorship, black writing and white writing. He always insists that he is merely a privileged participant in a historical process, and that *Skelm* is the creation of the black writers. This, paradoxically, confers additional esteem on him in some quarters, which in turn creates suspicion and envy in others. Though he insists on Mogorosi's presence at all interviews and never says I, only we, the Simon Sibandlas are determined to discredit him.

So far he has handled the situation with delicacy, but Ruth is concerned that he could be brought down by what might be his fatal flaw: he enjoys his public image. It would be unnatural if he did not. There is a constant stream of students, both male and female, who come to the office to offer their help in the production of *Skelm*, or bring contributions of poetry, photographs and graphics. The young women often emerge with an attractive flush on their faces; their offerings, whatever they are, have apparently been accepted. Nicholas is divorced. He married young, and after four years of marriage, he and his wife parted. Ruth knows as little of his personal life as he knows of hers. She understands that in Mogorosi's or Simon's scheme of things, he is expected to abdicate, soon, but she believes he should remain at the helm until Skelm Publications is properly established.

"Of course Skelm Publications is non-racial," Nicholas is saying to Simon, "but we'll be publishing mainly black writing, to redress the balance. Bring your next poetry collection to us, Simon," he adds with a degree of cunning that surprises Ruth.

"Huh! First you'll have to prove yourselves," Simon responds. "You may go bust and where will that leave me? Van Riebeecks have treated me fine. Royalties in time, promotion, everything. Besides, I'm an established writer, you can't compare me with the young ones. Anyway, who's interviewing whom?"

Mogorosi says something in Sotho and Simon laughs. "I don't say you're a worse writer than I am, Mogorosi. It's just that I've got standards, man."

Ruth is surprised he admits to standards. The blacks scoff at the term; white critics and academics lament its absence. Standards, say the latter, are being sacrificed to the sociological process. But Nicholas insists they are talking about different things: while white writers begin with the idea of excellence, black writing is an experiment in openness which fits in with the African oral tradition. It is a unique, cultural development, he says. The *Skelm* writers are called 'relevant', 'committed', 'non-elitist'. They not only write for the magazine; they also distribute it in the townships, where ninety per cent of *Skelm's* readership lives.

"Who makes decisions here, you or Mogorosi?" Simon is asking.

"I don't like the way you phrased that question," Mogorosi says angrily. "You know I don't work here, but I'm part of the editorial collective. We consult, we try to make decisions together. Not only Nicholas and myself. We try to draw in the rest of the staff as well as our writers."

"Like the white lady next door?" Simon raises his voice.

A chair is pushed back and angry whispers are exchanged. Nicholas comes through to Ruth's office but she does not look up; she is proof-reading. He rifles through some files in the cabinet, then goes out, closing the door behind him.

Ten minutes later the door opens. Simon comes out, calling over his shoulder, "Thank you very much, gentlemen and comrades-in-letters! And good luck in your future endeavours."

"Simon!" Nicholas hurries after him, carrying a manuscript wrapped in brown paper. "You once offered to read for us. This is a play about the 1976 uprising by someone who calls himself Nocha Nakasa. No one seems to know him. It might be the pseudonym of an exile or banned writer. There's no address, only post restante Rissik Street. Mogorosi's more enthusiastic about it than I am; too 'well-made' for me. Would you care to give us an opinion?"

Nocha Nakasa. Ruth is surprised at the Jewish-sounding name. She herself has not seen the manuscript.

"Nocha?" Simon takes the manuscript. "Sure. I'll read it this weekend. We must all make our little contribution, mustn't we?"

Ruth is acknowledged by Simon with a slight nod and self-satisfied smile as he goes through to the *Skelm* office where he is greeted with a loud "hey man!" by Jenny. She used to be Nicholas' assistant – and lover, Ruth guesses – but after a row which took place behind closed doors and from which Jenny emerged weeping, she moved in with Thami and Vusi whose office doubles as a club for the *Skelm* writers.

Vusi, whose job was created by everyone taking a cut in pay, acts more like a political commissar than an editor or proof-reader. A few weeks ago Nicholas had received an angry letter from a white poet, together with the rejection note sent by Vusi: "If you want to write for *Skelm,*" it read, "you must toe the line." Nicholas, after a long talk to Vusi, assured the poet that there had been a cross-cultural misunderstanding. In township jargon, he explained, toeing the line meant waiting in a queue.

"Fancy footwork," Ruth had commented. The writer thought so too; he withdrew his poem.

Ruth has not been writing. "You're being brow-beaten by the BC lobby," Sara says. "Your latest book is your best yet." But Ruth will not send it to the publishers. Simon is probably right: What do the whites really know about black suffering.

Daniel, on the other hand, is mildly surprised that she has stopped writing, but when she tries to explain how she feels, a veil of boredom shutters his eyes.

Once in six weeks she goes to meetings of the non-racial writers' group. They last for an hour or two, and leave her with the feeling that much of what is said has been rehearsed at cabals in the townships. Workshops are no longer mentioned, not even by David, who seems dispirited but continues to attend. "If my grandchildren ever ask what I did for the Revolution," he has told Ruth, "I shall say I saw four different versions of Thami's play." He has been trying to persuade Thami to shed his role as Soweto Renaissance Man, and concentrate his talents in one particular field, preferably not playwriting.

What David does not know is that Mogorosi arranges workshops in the townships to which white writers are not invited. Ruth has overheard Vusi discuss this with Mogorosi. She has not told David; she still hopes that the goodwill and enthusiasm of the young writers will prevail over ideology. In the meantime, *Skelm* remains an island on which meaningful literary contact between blacks and whites is still possible, and for that Ruth is grateful.

Sounds of merriment come from the *Skelm* office. Simon has left, but other callers have arrived.

Thami comes through to her office. He looks uncomfortable.

"That Simon," he says. "He's got a big wooden spoon and he likes to stir the pap. We are starting to workshop my new play on Wednesday night, Ruth. Can you come? I'd like to know what you think of it."

"Won't the others resent a white woman mixing in?" Ruth asks. She has been to rehearsals in Soweto many times, but lately she does not feel at ease at township gatherings.

"Ach no, man. They know you're a writer, a friend. Remember you said it was too static? I've added another character, someone who has returned secretly from exile..."

Ruth remains doubtful. "Perhaps not, Thami. Bring me the script. I'll see the play later."

She has come to know the young messengers, clerks and cleaners, the students and unemployed young blacks who come to the office. When Nicholas is too busy to see them, she puts aside her proofs and galleys, and together they go through a poem or a story. She is gentle but firm. It will be more powerful, she says, if you find the right word for the right idea, the right feeling. Listen to the township voices; that's where you'll find the words. And get to know your history, speak to the old people. You won't find it in the history books.

"Nicholas is busy," Ruth hears Jenny say. "I'll read the poem."

She, Thami and Vusi are supposed to make selections from the piles of poems and stories that come in from all over the country, edit them lightly, or send them back to the writers with suggestions for change. Thami is the only one who works hard. Vusi conducts political seminars, and Jenny spends more time socialising than working. Papers, galleys and made-up pages are scattered all over her desk, and at lunch time, greasy polystyrene containers drip curry and tomato sauce over proofs. She is a chain smoker, and there is always a smell of burned plastic and paper from the cigarettes she stubs out in the overflowing wastepaper baskets.

"Amazing!" Ruth hears Jenny exclaim. Her critical vocabulary is limited. "A-mazing! Vusi, have a squizz. Definitely for the next issue."

After the *Skelm* group leaves, Ruth packs her bag and goes in to say goodnight to Nicholas. He is writing something on a piece of paper. As she comes in, he slips it into a file.

"I hope it's a poem," she says.

"I've forgotten how to write poetry," he says. "It's the soccer team for Sunday's game."

"Soccer team?" Ruth laughs.

"Don't you know about our Lefties' League? We've got eight teams with names like Happy Warriors, most of whom are black; Gramsci on the Southern Question, with a political philosophy to match; Gumpertz, which is my team and don't ask me where we picked that name up; Crown Mines, and so on. This Sunday we're playing Crown Mines, and we've got to beat them. They usually wipe us up. They're young and fit and our team's a bunch of middle-aged academics, lawyers and journalists."

Ruth smiles. Nicholas is thirty-four.

"What do you mean, you've got to beat them? Where's your sportsmanship? May the best team win, and all that."

"Sportsmanship? That's bourgeois, imperialist. Everyone's out to win."

"Sounds rather unattractive."

He laughs. "I didn't think it would appeal to you. It's so difficult to make up a strong team." He takes out the list and frowns.

"What's the problem?" she asks. "No one want to play right wing?"

"Your cracks used to go over my head," he confesses. "You deliver your lines with such a straight face that one's first impulse is to explain things to you. Like when I told you that BC stood for Black Consciousness and was in no way related to Christ's birth day. Bloody patronising of me."

"You're forgiven. Anything urgent?"

"No. I feel bad you're working so hard. For books."

"Don't worry. I'm enjoying it."

"Simon's a tough nut," he goes on. "He says outrageous things but doesn't really mean them. After all, some of his best friends – and publishers – are white."

"You're beginning to make jokes yourself. I'm off. My daughter's coming to supper tonight. It's an occasion. Since she moved out , we have to make an appointment to see her."

"I've met Sara. She's a big soccer fan. Watches our matches every Sunday. Especially when Crown Mines is playing."

"It can't be our Sara. She's not a sports fan. She's one of those graceful but completely uncoordinated people who can't hit a ball over the net. And she hates watching sport."

"Michael introduced her as Sara Singer, so I assumed she was your daughter. I imagined a resemblance. If Michael weren't bigger, stronger and handsomer than me..."

"Michael? Michael who?" Ruth goes very still.

"Michael Stern."

"It adds up." She sits down.

"Are you all right, Ruth? You look as though you've seen a ghost."

"What's this ghost, this Michael, like?"

"Politically sound..."

"Baruch ha-Shem." Ruth holds her head between her hands.

"...Active in anti-conscription affairs and trade unions. I believe he's doing honours in industrial sociology. He's also a cartoonist and photographer. One of those disgusting all-rounders and goodlooking to boot. I'm sure you've seen him, Ruth. He's brought photographs to the office. In fact, we used one in the last issue. The one of the old man sleeping in the doorway, covered with newspapers."

"Can't recall. So many people come to the office." Ruth takes a deep breath and stands up. "I'll be on my way. See you tomorrow."

"Are you sure...?"

Ruth doesn't hear the rest of the sentence. She moves mechanically out of the building, into her car. Michael Stern, Michael Stern, Michael Stern. Retribution. Her mind goes around in circles. Only when she reaches the top of the Ridge, where the radio mast stands, does she become aware of her surroundings. She stops and gets out of the car. Except for the sound of distant traffic, there is silence. If she listens very carefully, she can hear the wind soughing through the dry autumn grass. Below are the pyramid roofs of the suburbs. During the day she can pick out the roof under which she lived as an adolescent. Across the golf course the lights of the Aged Home flicker through the trees, and to the far right is the open veld. Soon the veld fires will start again. One spark and the fire will fan out, blackening the veld, singeing the trees at its edges.

Behind her are the steps, cut into rock, which lead to the radio mast. At the end of World War II, a large cross had been erected on the same spot to celebrate VE day. For days the silence of the hills had been shattered by an insistent hammering, digging and scraping which echoed over the suburb without revealing its source. Then the metallic clanging stopped, and a tall cross had been raised. Not long afterwards, she and Paul had walked in these hills. He, the anthropology student, had shown her the Stone Age tools and the Iron Age ruins that lay scattered over the hills. He had told her about stronger cultures absorbing or destroying weaker cultures, and of new societies rising out of the ruins, only to be destroyed again. On a large, flat rock he had made an offering of a protea bud and a stone axe to the Ancestors, the ancient hill-dwellers. Forgive us, he had said with mock-religious fervour, for displacing you. You'll be avenged one day. Sometime afterwards she had married Daniel and they had emigrated to Israel. When they returned, they had built a house on the hill, not far from the ruins and the rock. The VE Day cross, by then, had been replaced by the radio mast. Paul never forgave her. You might have had the sensitivity to build your home elsewhere, he had said.

Ruth returns to the car, and drives a few metres down the road, into the garage, which is at street level. Daniel is not home yet, but in a corner of the garage she sees a motor cycle.

There is a flurry of footsteps and a dark figure emerges from the shrubs, running up the path. She stands still, holding her breath.

"Luke!" she says, with relief. "You gave me a fright. We haven't seen you for such a long time. How are you?"

"Awright." He stops a few feet away from her, not meeting her eyes. He is carrying a suitcase.

"Won't you come inside? I'd like to talk to you."

"Can't. Must go to catch the bus." His voice is rough, gritty, subdued.

"Well, some other time." She stands aside and he runs up the steps, disappearing into the dusky gloom.

Selina is waiting for her at the door. She has been crying.

"Did you see Luke?" she asks. Ruth nods. "Trouble again. He's out on bail. He's going home to my mother. Trouble, always trouble."

Ruth hears laughter as she comes into the house.

"Miss Sara," Selina explains. "She has been here now for a long time."

"That's funny. I didn't see her car," Ruth says, hanging her jacket on the hallstand.

"She came with," Selina lowers her head, "with her friend on the motor bike."

Ruth takes a deep breath and walks into the lounge.

"I thought you were never coming," Sara says as she kisses her. Her cheeks are flushed, her eyes shining.

My day for ghosts. Ruth watches a young Paul get up from the couch and come towards her, his hand outstretched.

"I'm Michael Stern," he says. As though he needs an introduction.

"And I'm Ruth Erlich, I mean Singer," she replies, reddening. It is a long time since she has thought of herself as Ruth Erlich.

He laughs, and Ruth, against her will, laughs too. "I would have recognised you anywhere," he says, "although Sara doesn't really look like you. I've been up to the *Skelm* offices but didn't seek you out. I was, uh, a little uncertain of my reception. Still am."

"Stay for supper," she says. Behind his charm, she senses a resoluteness that frightens her a little. She stills her qualms: she has never seen Sara look so radiant.

"Thank you. If Mr Singer won't mind."

"I'm not sure of anything any more," Ruth says. "Does, uh, do your parents, are your parents aware of your friendship with Sara?"

"Not yet. Sara said we should try it out on you first. She thought it might be easier."

"I'm not sure what gives her that confidence."

"Our motto; let live. Don't let me down."

"Don't count on that. When I leave this room, I'll probably fall down in a dead faint."

Ruth feels trapped in a time warp. The Dispossessed, she thinks as she goes out of the lounge, are exacting revenge, both for themselves and for Paul, who at least propitiated them with a protea bud. Serves her right for building on a sacred site; serves her right for betraying the heart.

TWELVE

16 December 1980

Dear Jeanne,

Before defending myself against your accusation that I'm so obsessed with a certain hatred from my youth that I'm prepared to sacrifice my children on its altar, I want to give you a short sketch of a day in the life of a white South African woman. I imagine your impatient shrug: I know it all, idiot mother; that's why I left the country. You don't know it all, my dear Jeanne; not even we who stayed on know it all. On the surface everything seems calm, ordinary, but there is a kind of electricity in the air, a rumbling beneath the earth, a sense of impending disaster, but nobody knows where or how it will erupt. Bear with me for a page or two. It may help put things into perspective, both for me and for you.

One morning, a few weeks ago, I woke to the sound of Philemon cleaning. He banged and he slammed and he clattered, chanting what sounded like a Zulu war cry in a restrained yet highly audible bass. In the kitchen, Grace was preparing breakfast. Dishes rattled, pots clanked, chairs were scraped across the tiles and the kettle whistled frantically; all

99

to make two cups of coffee and a few slices of buttered toast. (The trials and burdens of a White Madam!) Your father, in the meantime, had wired himself to every electrical appliance he could muster: his shaver, electric toothbrush, walkman, and so on. I had gone to bed late the previous night after a vain effort to cope with the correspondence. I had hoped I might lie in for a while, but gave up and promised myself an early night. If I survived the day. Which I almost did not.

I drove into town, got parking outside Joubert Park, and saw the meths drinkers slouching around the gates after a night out on the concrete under newspaper, their hands blue, their feet filthy, purple-nosed and bleary-eyed, a dramatic contrast to the neatly dressed black workers who were arriving in Combis from the townships. The Noord Street bus terminus was also teeming with black people, many of whom stopped to buy fruit at the stalls near the buses. I walked past the large butcher shop on the corner and was unwise enough to look into the window. There, on a large white enamel tray, lay sheep's heads with closed eyes and bloody necks. I should've recognised a bad omen and returned immediately to the safety of my home in the white suburbs. But I did not. I gagged and walked on, past the chemist shop with twenty kinds of skin lighteners; past the cafe where people were eating samosas, sipping maas and drinking Coke, and past the clothing shop where a droopy-eyed black man stood, holding a petticoat in one hand and a skirt in the other, saying, 'cheap, cheap, cheap,' like some unhappy, captive bird. All along the pavement medicine men sat at their trestle tables, displaying herbs, barks and roots, the skin and bones of all sorts of animals, and goodness knows what else, I'm always too squeamish to look. The mealie vendors squatted beside their hessian sacks, wrapped in their blankets, holding up a few partially peeled mealies whose kernels gleamed like dentures through the pale green leaves and silky tassles. On my way home, I decided, I'd buy some mealies for Philemon and Grace. Philemon is especially fond of them. When he first came to work for us, he planted mealies in the rose bed and

I hadn't had the heart to pull them up. Thus far, an ordinary day in the centre of Johannesburg, which increasingly is looking like the very heart of Africa.

Have patience, Jeanne; this is not a literary exercise. I'm trying to reconstruct the frame of mind which led me to act, as you put it, in such an irrational and obsessed manner later that morning.

As I turned the corner and saw the police vehicle, I realised it was not going to be an ordinary day after all. A Yellow-Mellow – as the township kids call these monstrous police vans – was parked opposite our building, and behind it was a row of yellow and blue police cars. Police officers were leaning against them, waiting, some with walkie-talkies in their hands, others with fingers looped through their belts from which gun holsters hung. What's happening, I asked one of the blacks who was standing on the pavement. It's the first of May, he reminded me. The Unions are having a meeting inside the hall, and the police are waiting for them to come out. Then I heard a voice over the megaphone inside the building: Amandla! and the answering roar, Ngwethu! One speech over, another began. When they come out, the man next to me said, it will be bang, bang, bang, no questions asked. But it's not illegal to have a meeting inside a building, I said. It doesn't have to be illegal, he answered politely, and moved off.

I worked my way through the crowds and went into the building. Nothing was apparently going to happen until the meeting was over. The Amandlas were coming thick and fast. In the vestibule, under the weary eyes of Christ-on-the-tapestry, were trestle tables with books and pamphlets. I went upstairs. Nobody was working. Both counsellors and supplicants were crowded around the windows, looking on to the street below. I made a call to the Campus Law Clinic to ask if they would handle two prisoners' pleas for legal aid. Send the letters on to us, I was told, and we'll see what we can do. I put them into an envelope with a covering note, then joined the people at the windows.

The police officers seemed quite relaxed. They were still

leaning against their cars, watching the building. Two fat men in safari suits, cameras in hand, were taking pictures of everyone who went into or came out of our building. As I leaned out of the window, one of the men turned his camera on me. I'm afraid I acted childishly; I made a moue at him. (Sorry, Jeanne. French again. You've made me self-conscious about using French expressions which come naturally to me. I am NOT showing off.) Then there was a bit of comic relief. A black man in baggy green pants, wearing a jacket too large for him and a squashed hat on his head, lunged out of the crowd, with a large paper-bag in his hand. The officers tensed momentarily, then realised he was drunk. Standing about three feet away from them, he put the paper-bag into his left hand, and saluted them with his right, at the same time clicking his right leg against his very unstable left leg, almost toppling over. All the bystanders laughed. One of the officers said, voetsek bliksem, and the man moved off, smiling. I wondered how drunk he was. All amiable so far, except that the crowd had been enlarged by people on their way from the Noord Street bus terminus, and by a TV crew and photographers who had emerged from nowhere. Everyone stood around, waiting.

Then the singing began. *Nkosi Sikele iAfrica.* End of meeting. A police officer lifted the walkie talkie to his mouth, and there was a sound of heavy motors revving up. Leaning further out of the window I saw that both ends of the street were being blocked off by police trucks. Police began moving in with their dogs, dispersing the black spectators, leaving a few whites, the TV crew and the photographers. In the momentary silence that followed, I heard the clip-clop of boots, and leaning forward at a precarious angle, I saw what looked like a corps de ballet running down the centre of the street: riot police in helmets, wearing light grey shirts and dark grey trousers, hunched, their weapons held down in front of them, forming a perfectly straight line and observing an exact distance between each other. If they hadn't, they would have poked their guns into one another's backsides. They'd been disgorged from one of those yellow trucks that was closing off the street. An officer, unarmed, barked out commands to which they responded like automatons. They stopped, one facing the building, the next turning to the opposite side of the street, guns at the ready. Another command and they formed a semi-circle around the entrance to Khotso House, closing off the entrance. Just then we heard the hall doors swing open, and people began pouring into the vestibule, toyi-toyiing and singing. Two of our black translators were standing on either side of me at the window, ululating, singing and chanting – We are not afraid! We are not afraid! in unison with the crowd downstairs. I was afraid. Terrified. I had a premonition of disaster. I shut my eyes and saw the white enamel tray with the lambs' heads.

Voices were coming over megaphones, from inside and outside the building, but I couldn't hear what they were saying. Later I learned that the trade unionists had appealed to the police to allow the people to disperse quietly, and the police had ordered them to come out one at a time and not to congregate around the entrance. At the time it sounded like a declaration of war. I was certain there was going to be a massacre.

I looked down at the swelling crowd below, and among them, camera in hand, photographing both the riot squad and the people coming out of the building, was Michael. Next to him was a girl with long blond hair, holding his camera bag. Michael! I shrieked, but he couldn't hear me. I pushed my way down the steps into the vestibule where I got caught up in the dancing, chanting crowd. They looked ecstatic, mesmerised, ready to face the firing squad outside. Don't go! I wanted to shout, but the words stuck in my throat. I had one thought in mind: I had to get to Michael. I rushed downstairs, fought my way out of the doors, and was momentarily stopped by the sight of the riot police at the bottom of the steps, their visors dropped over their faces, their guns pointed at the entrance to the building. I don't know what they thought when they saw fat, grey, tearstained woman rushing out of the building, and

I cared even less. But I controlled myself: Excuse me, I said politely, and moved around them to an opening at the edge of the steps, where I saw Michael, kneeling, shooting away with his camera.

I know. You'd have died of mortification. I think Michael also suffered a minor death, and have no doubt he'd have loved to inflict one on me. At first he didn't see me: this was a man at work. The girl and I looked at one another, hard. It was instant recognition: she looks like her but has his colouring. I'd have known her anywhere. She smiled, a little shakily, but held it, and looked me straight in the eye. Michael stood up, took in the scene, then said, "Gee, Ma, thanks for coming to my rescue."

You know the rest; you got it straight from the horse's mouth – and from his blinkered point of view. I didn't make a scene – another one, that is. I didn't say anything. I just walked away. No one was hurt. The blacks were allowed to leave peacefully. This time. As for the rest of us, well...

On my way back to the car I bought half a dozen mealies from one of the vendors. She wrapped them in a piece of newspaper. 'Revolution is their objective', was the headline. Perhaps they're right.

Michael has no doubt written that he was civilly received in the Singer household, and that their private misgivings, if any, were not aired in his presence. They apparently have this alliterative family motto which runs something like Let Live, Loz Leben, Laat Lewe. Very civilised. But I, too, have a right to be left alone, and to chose whom I see and whom I invite to my home. And that girl is not one of them.

Another thing: it's not true that Michael has always been my favourite child. I love you equally, in different ways. Chantal and I, for example, write to one another about children and husbands, homes and cooking and her reactions to her new life in a new country. You chose not to write about your personal emotions. All I know is that you and Clive have broken off, but I don't know if you've met anyone else and I don't ask, though I'd like to know, naturally. I know that you're getting on very well in your Modern Dance Group and I'm happy about that. Then again, I never write about my political activities, such as they are, to Chantal. Believe me, I'd have been just as shocked had either you or Chantal got involved with one of the Singers. Call it irrational, call it what you will: Ruth Singer is my bête noire (and I'm not apologising this time!) and there is nothing I can do about it. Hyper-sensitivity? Well, you don't have a monopoly on that. Remember your exaggerated reaction when I mentioned anorexia nervosa to you a few months ago?

Dad has just looked over my shoulder and said, you have a genius for alienating your children; you're becoming more like your mother every day. And I know how he felt about my mother! He, of course, is lapping all this up. At last he and his son have something in common: the Singer women. I haven't cut Michael out of my will, as you put it. He still comes here as seldom as possible, usually when Zalman visits. He seems to have more to say to Zalman than he does to either me or Dad. We talk and argue as always, but I've made it perfectly clear that I do not want to meet Sara, and that's that.

My work, at least, gives me some satisfaction. I've recently joined a women's group who are planning a series of protests against the imprisonment of black children for the heinous crimes of boycotting school or throwing stones when the police scale the school fences to break up meetings. We meet in that chapel in our building. Recently we've been joined by a few black women from the townships. One of them, Agnes, seems very militant. She is quite a striking woman: very dark-skinned, marvellous white teeth, scarlet finger and toe nails that seem to glow against her velvety black skin. She's always urging us on to action, but we're still at the planning stage.

I'm still doing the correspondence, but that's very depressing. It seems there's little the lawyers can do about the letters prisoners smuggle out of jail. Today I'm sending you excerpts from a very different kind of letter. I still haven't worked out an answer to it.

Dear Madams,

I was working at the C Hotel for three years together with M.T... She told me one day that I must be a fortuner. Every time she was telling me that I must be a fortuner. She first gave me a bottle sea water with sand and tied with a piece of wool. She said one day to me you know I have two sisters staying in Town and they dont want me, they say that I am a wizard ... October November Desember I was at M.T's place at Zone 1 D No.–. She said to me you are going to be born new. She killed me before. She asked me where did you go to the witch docter? She asked me becaus she find her self guilty of wat she was doing to me. She put me outside in the night. There are people in the night around in the house whom she had killed. They work in the night when she sleep. They get up and make some porridge to eat. They say to the people, dumela, say yes. If you say yes that means you say yes I want to die. Too manny people are dying. She was calling me my friend all the time ... In the night she fly and she take people to fly ... She took my watch, panty, shoes, peticoat, baking pans, sizzer ... She eat blood. She always say she need blood. She want blood. Every month every week people are dying and getting lost all over the world. If you bury people they come in the night and dig. People are afraid of her ... She send other people to work for her. She turn to be a snake in the night. They start to say kill all the god of water all over the world. They are sent to steel some muti wearing musk and some gloves ... Is better if they make a surch at D Zone to make proof...

She took even my clothes, many things. She worked me with electricity. I am like TV F.M. She make me sethotsela. I need help ... She killed us all in the house, even all the world. She is doing all this things killing people, sending bad air to the world. She is the course of all this damages all over the world...

Well, Jeanne. Be thankful for small mercies. At least I don't ride around on a broomstick or stick pins into dolls marked

R.S. – even if you do think I'm an old witch.
I miss you so much. Let's be friends. Love, Ma.

P.S. Don't get me wrong: I'm very upset about the Michael/
Sara matter; I don't want to alienate Michael and it's not the
girl's fault that she is who she is. On a rational level I know
what I should do, but can't act on it.
P.P.S. An interesting insight has emerged from my brush
with our armed forces: When I'm angry enough, I lose my
fear. I felt I could take on the whole riot squad that morning.
But I'm not brave enough to take on Sara.

THIRTEEN

On the evening of the apotheosis of Nocha Nakasa, Ruth returns from the writers' meeting to an empty house. Daniel is away on business and Selina has gone to her room. She eats the dry-edged veal and glassy potatoes Selina has left for her in the warmer, then walks on to the verandah. It is a still, warm evening with a crescent moon floating in the deep black sky. The twinkling suburban lights eclipse the stars which recede into space, drawing her with them. She clings to the rough bark of the tamarisk tree, resisting the pull, waiting for her dizziness to pass. She has seldom felt so alone, so desolate.

The meeting at the *Skelm* office, earlier in the evening, had seemed no different from any other in the last eighteen months: the same messy room, the same dog-eared photographs on the walls, the same black writers, the same white writers: David, Nicholas, Jenny and herself. Thami and his friends had stood around in groups, talking and laughing; Ma-Deborah was lecturing Nkatsana, immaculately dressed in a floral German print, and Jenny, in her grubby jeans, was acting the hostess, slapping shoulders and giving the African handshake: thumbs, palms, thumbs. Mandla Magwaza, surrounded by a group of admirers, was reciting his latest poem, looking to David for approval. And Simon, normally a reluctant participant at these gatherings, seemed unusually alert. He stood in a corner, speaking eagerly in a low voice to Mogorosi.

"Before we begin," said Vusi, chairman for the evening, "Simon would like to say a few words."

"This," Simon announced, holding up a red file, "marks the rise of a new black star. It is written by a real artist, probably an exile, who calls himself Nocha Nakasa. For all we know, he may even be related to the late great Nat When Nicholas asked me to read it, I thought, yet another book. But it's more than just another book; it is a landmark in black writing in South Africa. Nakasa writes about the '76 uprising from the inside – one can recognise first-hand experience – and he exposes the false liberalism of the whites in a devastating manner. He's proof we don't need their patronage and their workshops. Publish it soon, Nicholas," he had added. "Let us show the world..."

Ruth had sat very still, her eyes shut, hoping to wake from her nightmare. When she opened them, Simon was still holding the red file, lauding Nocha Nakasa, railing against white elitists. She had forgotten that Sara had taken the manuscript from her; she had even forgotten Sara's anger when Ruth refused to have it published. "We have no right to colonise the blacks' suffering," she had told Sara. "You used to talk about imagination, about excellence," Sara had replied, "now you pussyfoot around, trying to pretend literature doesn't exist." "Let's say we disagree on this," Ruth had answered, "just as we do about your moving in with Michael."

Sara, no doubt, had sent the manuscript to Nicholas as a prank, certain it would not go beyond his desk; she had wanted to make a point. Now Simon, of all people, was making it for her. Ruth should have been alerted when Nicholas told Simon the author's name. Nocha Nakasa, she remembered thinking; sounds Jewish to me. Another Nakasa indeed. Then she had put it out of her mind.

"You can't publish it," she told Nicholas after the meeting.

"Can't publish it?" He had laughed. "Another of your enigmatic jokes. Not only will we publish it; Thami will stage it for the Laager."

One look at her face told him the whole story.

"How could you do this to me?" he had groaned, sinking into his chair, head in hands, elbows on the desk. "How could you have played such a sick, dangerous joke? Do you realise this can break up the group? Oh God, you've ruined years of work, years of building up credibility."

Gone was the charismatic, imaginative rider of the Zeitgeist. Before her sat a wiry, fair-haired young man with a passion for football who did not like losing matches, let alone being disqualified for foul play; the hero who had scored the goals but given the credit to his team.

As she watched culture hero metamorphose into football player, Ruth forgot, temporarily, how mightily Nicholas had laboured to produce *Skelm,* to maintain a balance between white and black writers and to ward off the censorship board and their minions. He had even given up his own writing to produce a forum for black writers. But he, too, had diminished her: how could he have imagined, after all those months of working together, that she, so conscious of the sensitive situation, would play such a potentially destructive joke?

"If the book's so good," was all she had said as she walked out of his office, "publish it, under any name you please."

My life, she thought as Nicholas shrank to human dimensions, is littered with clay feet. Would she never outgrow her need for a knight on a white horse, a chalutz on a tractor, a rider on the Zeitgeist? Serves her right for harbouring messianic longings. Why can't she accept that life has no meaning, no purpose; that one has to seize it, live by the day, and be grateful for a sunset, a bird-song, a flower?

She had grown up hearing about pogroms, the Holocaust, slavery and oppression. Her uncle Berka's family had been slaughtered by the Cossacks; her father's by the Nazis. Had there been a God, she used to hear them say, such catastrophes would never have happened. So she learned to live without

God. But she could not live without faith in love, in people, in justice. She set out on a lifelong quest, a pilgrimage, for love, for justice, following false messiahs and taking paths that led to disillusion. Knights, she realised at an early age, had not been chivalrous or romantic. They had locked their ladies into chastity belts and ridden off in pursuit of the 'infidel', that is, anyone with different religious beliefs. Exit Prince Valiant, enter Hagar the Horrible. Chalutzim, it took her longer to understand, created insular, model villages, not a new society. And the Zeitgeist, it was now reaffirmed, cannot be harnessed, no matter how imaginative or skilful its rider.

People, it seems, will not or cannot fit into Procrustean moral structures – including chastity belts – designed for them by rogues or ideologues. She is uncertain whether this is a hopeful sign, or whether human beings are too base to aspire to higher things.

She must speak to Sara, she remembers, releasing her hold on the tamarisk tree. If Sara hasn't the sense to realise what disastrous results her injudicious prank can cause, Ruth will have to spell it out for her.

Michael answers the phone. Even his voice is like Paul's. "Hello, Mrs, uh," he begins.

They seldom speak on the phone, nor has he been back to the house since his first visit. "I'm not going to subject him to your unfriendly behaviour," Sara had said to Daniel afterwards. He had greeted Michael coolly, then taken refuge behind his newspaper. "Have some humility. It is not Michael who created the havoc in your lives. Let live indeed. The lip service you pay to freedom," she added bitterly. Daniel had been taken aback by Sara's attack. When she visits, always alone, and not very often, they hardly speak to one another.

"Please, call me Ruth," she tells Michael. "How are you?"

"I'm well, but much too busy."

"Michael, I've wanted to say this before. Don't be angry with Daniel. He didn't mean to be rude. I think he was a little overwhelmed, surprised, to meet you. He had no idea ... Come to dinner one evening with Sara."

"Thank you, I will. Let me call Sara; she's in the loo. Sara!"

So intimate, so domestic. In the loo. Exact location. Stop it, Ruth tells herself. Accept it. Sara has never been so happy. Let her enjoy it, while it lasts.

Sara is unrepentant when Ruth describes the events of the evening. "I had not intended anyone but Nicholas to read it," she confirms Ruth's guess. "But this is even better. Why can't you all get together and have a good laugh about it? And when you're finished laughing, get down to the nitty-gritty of opening up the literary scene in a totally colour-blind way."

"Apparently this isn't the correct historical season for laughter," Ruth says drily. She can imagine Simon rolling about with merriment, shrieking, Simple Simon! I've been duped! I've been duped!

"You used to say one could laugh at anything, anytime," Sara replies. "However, I'll phone Nicholas right now and tell him why I did it. I don't have to be over-delicate with him. You should see what an aggressive little bugger he is on the soccer field. Michael had a huge bruise on his thigh last soccer season, and it wasn't an accident."

"I'm sure he's recovered. Goodnight, Sara," she says. "I'm going to bed."

"Wait, you remember what Michael said about the *Skelm* people, especially Mogorosi and Simon? So don't be taken in by their sob stories of their isolation in the townships because they belong to a non-racial group. They're a bunch of racists themselves who are slowly losing their support among the people. The ANC is gaining ascendancy..."

"I'm sure Michael knows what's happening in the townships. I don't know what Simon's up to, nor Mogorosi for that matter, but I'm sure the others are keen to continue their working relationship with white writers. Sara, I'm too tired to discuss this. Be well. And come soon. With Michael."

She slumps down on the sofa. Laugh yourselves out of it indeed. Ruth cannot remember when she herself last enjoyed a hearty belly-laugh, or even a spontaneous burst of laughter. She makes jokes, all right, cutting jokes with a bitter edge, but she has forgotten what joyous laughter sounds like.

She and Daniel had laughed a great deal in the early years, especially when the children were small. But the laughter had dried up, together with their love. They had remained together even after that tangle of love and betrayal with Lola and Paul, partly because neither knew how to dismantle a relationship that went back to their childhood. She was shrivelling to dust in the desert of her emotions; he found other ways of coping. She had seen lipstick on his collars, smelled perfume on his shirts. She remembered, with wonder, the searing jealousy of her youth and marvelled at its absence. She had always wanted to live passionately, fully, open to experience. Instead she had been sucked into a domestic trap, finding release only through her writing. Give me strength, she has appealed to the empty heavens time and time again, to tell Daniel we must part, that our relationship is dead. But she always finds reasons for delaying it. First the children were too young; then she did not want to disrupt their studies; now Daniel is going through a crisis at work. The only way we'll part, she thinks as she climbs wearily into bed, is when we're dead.

When Ruth arrives at work the following morning, Nicholas looks sheepish, embarrassed. She wonders what Sara said to him the previous evening. He apologises for his outburst and explains, quite unnecessarily, the tensions under which he is working at the moment.

"Don't worry about a thing," he adds with a conspiratorial smile. "I'm about to receive a letter from Nocha Nakasa, post-marked London, saying he's withdrawing his book. He's having it published overseas." Nicholas smiles, pleased with his ingenious footwork. Ruth also smiles, wearily.

"When's your next football match?" she asks.

"It's summer. We don't play soccer in summer."

He looks puzzled. She picks up a set of galleys from his desk and returns to her office.

What neither he nor Ruth could have foreseen, as they limped away from the Nocha Nakasa débâcle, was that in a few weeks' time his team would move into a different league.

FOURTEEN

The motion to dissolve the non-racial writers' organisation came up within weeks of the Nocha Nakasa incident, at a meeting in the *Skelm* office. It began, like all other meetings, with talk, laughter, and the beating of drums. When everyone settled down, David came straight to the point.

"Why," he asked, "have our activities ground to a virtual halt? No poetry readings in the townships, no sign of the much-discussed workshops. If there are readings in the townships, white members haven't been told. What's going on?"

"Well," Thami twisted uncomfortably in his chair, "all sixteen township-based groups have been suffering from harassment by the police..."

"Tell me another, Thami. We've been to readings in the townships when Casspirs and Hippos have rumbled through the streets."

"We've been having other troubles," Ma-Deborah broke the silence that descended on the group. "I was summoned to a meeting of black journalists and told either to join their union or to form a black writers' union of our own: They don't want us to work with non-racial groups. And who will publish my books, I asked them. It's time we had our own publishers, they told me; the whites don't understand the Struggle."

"Ja, man," Thami added. "It's getting harder for the *Skelm* people. In the beginning we were asked to read our poems at the protest meetings. Now they boycott us. When the white members came to the townships for poetry readings, the BC people ostracised us. We didn't want to upset you, so we just stopped asking you to readings. There's this pressure..."

"Pressure, what pressure? Who's pressurising?" Simon shouted. Thami withdrew in surprise. "You've got it all wrong. The people in the townships feel this is not the time to fraternise with whites and we must respect their wishes. I am about to put a motion to this meeting that we disband this organisation."

"Disband?" Nicholas said, bewildered and dismayed. Mogorosi avoided his appealing glance.

"Disband?" David echoed. "What kind of solution is that? Since when do you do the government's dirty work for them? Do you realise this is one of the few places where whites and blacks can still meet on an equal basis?"

Simon heaved himself out of the chair. "In times like these," he boomed, "when the armed forces of South Africa are attacking our brothers in Mozambique, we cannot be in the same organisation with whites. Their interests are different from ours, and at this stage, for historical and political reasons, polarisation is inevitable and necessary. That is why we want to disband the group. Not because we are being pressurised by anyone." He glared at Thami.

"How can you associate that despicable raid on Mozambique with this literary group, and call for polarisation?" David asked. "Surely it's obvious which side we're on?" If it was, no one leapt up to affirm it. Thami lowered his head and intertwined his fingers; Vusi kept his eyes on Simon, a stiff smile on his lips, and Mogorosi, at this point, drew out a sheet of paper from his file.

"We propose," he said, "to call a general meeting of all

members at which we'll take a vote on whether or not to disband. Vusi has prepared this letter..."

And now representatives of writers' groups from all over the country are gathering at the Laager Theatre where they will debate Simon Sibandla's motion to disband the writers' organisation. Among them Ruth recognises aspiring poets who had brought their poems to the *Skelm* office on scraps of paper and in old exercise books, or had stood up in church halls to declaim, in ringing voices, their determination to be free and to liberate their people. With words. She will miss them all.

"I can't believe this is happening," David says as he and Ruth walk into the theatre. "But the venue does provide a delicious irony. From Shakespeare House, where it all began about two years ago, to the Laager, where it's about to end; from the bête blanc of black writers, to the last resort of nationalists, of all hues."

"Talking of beginnings and endings, there's Mandla." Ruth waves to him. "Without his drums and flowing robes, he looks like a general in mufti. I'll miss him. 'Africa my beginning, and Africa my ending'. Do you think he was influenced by Eliot?"

"Who knows? It may just be one of those antonymous couplings that suggest themselves to wordsmiths. What bets," David lowers his voice, "that our black friends will form their own writers' organisation before our multi-coloured body is cold?"

"David! You know what the problem is."

"I only know what I was told at our last meeting: Black Consciousness is now the dominating ideology in the townships, the ANC has lost ground, and their non-racial policies have been discredited. So BC groups are giving the *Skelm* people a hard time. The question is: are they the victims or are they the instigators?"

"The victims, naturally. Thami says life's become untenable in the townships. They're excluded from community events..."

"Yes, yes. For Thami life may be difficult. Not for Simon

and not for Mogorosi. You've read the preface to the stories Mogorosi's edited for Skelm Publications. He recommends peeing, spitting and shitting on literary convention, and kicking literature in the direction the blacks alone will determine, which won't be in the Great Tradition of the white colonialists. And who says it should be, for goodness sake? They've got their own literary tradition from which the young writers have been cut off by bannings, exile and a rotten educational system. The young ones believe they're creating black literature anew. That's why I wanted those workshops. They need to read Peter Abrahams, Mphahlele, Serote, Nkosi, Can Themba, Nat Nakasa. We're supposed to be fellow writers, fighting apartheid and censorship, not each other. I'm surprised Nicholas published Mogorosi's preface."

"Well, Simon told Nicholas..."

"Talk about the devil."

Simon walks into the theatre, an African print shirt hanging loosely over his belly. She half-expects him to strut up to her and say, "She insulted us! Made fools of us..." But Simon, even in the unlikely event that he knows who Nocha Nakasa is, has more solemn work in hand. He nods to her and David, then joins Mogorosi at the other end of the theatre.

"You're making it sound so sinister, David. They are experiencing difficulties."

"Your naivety would be charming, Ruth, if it weren't downright alarming. Has it ever occurred to you that we were being used, and that we're about to be dumped because we're no longer necessary?"

"You're either paranoid or over-simplifying, David. I can understand your feelings of outrage, but I don't believe it was a deliberate deception. Circumstances..."

Even as she says it, she thinks of the workshops to which white writers had not been invited; the hushed talks between Mogorosi and Vusi; Vusi's letter of rejection to the white poet who had not 'toed the line'; Mogorosi playing political commissar to Nicholas' imaginative publisher. David, after all, may not be paranoid.

She greets some of the white writers who are coming into the theatre, their funeral orations tucked into their pockets. They had been either wiser or less dedicated to a non-racial writers' group than she, David and a few others. They had dropped out at an early stage.

"Perhaps they're right," David says. "It's easy for us to be idealistic. We've had a privileged education; laws are made to protect Us from Them, and after our non-racial meetings, we return to our comfortable white suburbs. We are separate."

"Does that mean you're going to vote for dissolution?" Ruth asks.

"No! We've got to work together, otherwise there's no hope at all. Are you going to vote for disbandment?"

"Yes," Ruth replies, without conviction. "They have to shake off what they perceive as their colonial yoke – us."

"Then let them leave. Why should we disband?"

"To show solidarity."

"With an inverted racist stand? There's a corollary to this act of hara-kiri," David says. "If this isn't the time to work together, it's certainly not the time to live together. I shall emigrate, to Lapland or Lettland, or to any other place where one can live and Lett live. Okay, okay! I get carried away by words!"

"I shall go to Safad." Ruth has not thought about Safad for years. "Do you know that painting was my first love? When I was a child I had an uncle by marriage, Berka, whose walls I papered with drawings of feelings I could not express in words. I'm sick of words. I'll start painting again. I'll get a small studio in Safad, high up in the hills, where the air is clear and the light mysterious ... And perhaps my neighbour will be a tall, greying artist with whom I'll sit on the terrace after a day's work, sip wine, eat olives, and watch the sun set behind the hills..." She has learned nothing from experience.

"I've just realised," David says, looking at her, "how little we really know one another. All we've ever talked about is black writers and white writers. We've never even had an affair, though Rina thinks we have. What a waste. Is it too late?"

Ruth laughs. "It would have been a waste of a good friendship," she says. "But thanks for the offer, if it was an offer.

Here comes Nicholas, deep in conversation with Thami."

"How's he taking this?" David asks. "He works so hard at effacing his white face that one never knows what he really feels or thinks."

"He wants to hand over *Skelm* to Mogorosi, Thami and the others. He says he's done what he can and now it's over to them. He'll go back to teaching."

"In other words, he agrees with the BC stand."

"I don't know. He speaks about historical necessity."

"Hysterical necessity, the last refuge of rogues and liars, a cliché much loved by toers of lines. There's only one necessity: to be honest. I'm wary of people who speak about historical necessity."

Thami leaves Nicholas and comes across to David and Ruth.

"Heroic," David mutters. "Can he afford to be seen talking to us?" But he shakes Thami's hand warmly.

"Thanks for reading my poem," Thami says. "Your comments are very helpful, as usual. I'm reworking it."

"What do you think," David waves his arms in all directions, "about this?"

"It does not mean we can't be friends," Thami says. "It's just, it's just that the time isn't right..."

"Bullshit," David says.

"You have the poet's gift for the appropriate word," Ruth says.

Mogorosi calls the meeting to order, outlines the reasons for the Executive's recommendation, and for the next three hours, the same arguments are rehashed in varying degrees of calm, anger and sadness.

"Why," asks a white novelist who has not been to meetings for many months, "should the group disband? Let those who wish to withdraw do so, and let the others remain."

"If black writers remain," Mogorosi says, "they will have trouble in their communities. We have to make a choice, take a joint stand."

"If you all withdraw," another writer observes, "the group becomes a white organisation. This was to have been an experiment in non-racial co-operation. We might as well disband."

Although the gathering is dominated by those who wish to disband, there are a few dissident voices.

"The integrated Teachers' Association," says an Indian writer, "is enjoying support for its meetings in the townships. We haven't encountered opposition to a non-racial organisation. Why should the writers be having this trouble?"

"Teachers," says Mogorosi with a smile, "are not regarded as leader figures in the community. Writers are."

"Elitists," David says through clenched teeth.

"It is defeatist to disband," says a sociologist, the author of several learned texts, who has not been seen since the inaugural meeting in Shakespeare House. "Writers all over the world are under pressure from their societies. The black writers should not bow to pressure. They should show greater courage in facing it."

"Noble sentiments," David explodes, "from a white academic. But hardly appropriate and grossly insensitive under the circumstances."

Approval from Mogorosi is the last thing David seeks, but he gets it; a nod of assent. Mogorosi, however, finds it more difficult to still the dissident voice of Zuma, a black writer from Natal who, in addition to having an impeccable political record, is also a respected poet.

"Let us call things by their right names," Zuma says. "Black Consciousness is a positive force, a vehicle for regaining our knowledge of who we are, of valuing ourselves and our experience. We should accept and recognise this. It is a true reflection of our time and tries to do away with false cultural images imposed on us by whites. We are striving to slough off our servitude to white values and experience, but we are not anti-white, racist. What we must remember is that BC is not an end in itself; it is merely a stage in our struggle for liberation."

This is greeted with thunderous applause which Simon tries to stop. He stands up and shouts something about disruptive forces.

"What I mean," Zuma says calmly, with dignity, "is that further discussion of these issues is necessary before big decisions are taken. People are not speaking out, and I have an idea that the disbandment is being pushed from the outside. Something is being hidden. We are trapped in our class interests and don't know how to move forward, so we talk of colour, and we are saying racist things."

"It is not only a question of colour," Mogorosi says, controlling his anger with difficulty. "We are simply following what the community wants."

"And how," Zuma asks, "does one gauge what the community really wants? Perhaps the community is being pressed into thinking in a certain way. If writers are indeed leader figures, as Mogorosi suggests, they should try to give people both sides of the problem, especially if they are being led in the direction of racism."

"Sanity," David whispers to Ruth. "And unlike our esteemed sociologist, he's got a right to talk. He was a member of the ANC before it was banned and he's been arrested, banned and harassed all his life. I'm surprised he's still around."

Nicholas shows renewed interest in the debate now that Zuma has entered it.

"The Executive," he says, "had felt that there was sufficient feeling and reason for disbanding. This does not bind any member from voting against disbandment. Many new issues are coming to light at this meeting that hadn't been known before and this could influence the views held previously."

Delighted as Ruth is that Nicholas, at last, is showing fight, she knows it has come too late to mobilise real opposition. Mogorosi and Simon are determined to steamroller the meeting towards disbandment.

"The real question," says Mogorosi, "is: are we for the people or not? We have a strategy for handling pressure in the townships, but cannot do so while we are members of this organisation. We have to stand with the community. And now I think it is time to vote."

There are fifteen votes for disbandment, nine against and three abstentions. David has voted against, Nicholas for, and Ruth has abstained.

"As fellow writers," Mogorosi winds up the meeting, "we

hope to meet again when the situation is conducive."

"We shall regret this decision," Zuma predicts as he stands up to leave the theatre. "It has pushed back progress for a decade."

Nicholas stands alone, isolated. An enthusiastic group of young blacks has crowded around Mogorosi and Simon. As Nicholas picks up his papers and walks out of the theatre, Ruth makes an involuntary move towards him, but holds back.

"Another experiment that failed," David says as he and Ruth walk towards the car park. "I was wrong to have expectations. Perhaps non-racial co-operation isn't possible in an apartheid society. Perhaps even our views of literature are too different to reconcile. They emphasise the collective, we the individual. The result of this meeting can give comfort only to Treurnicht and his gauleiters. Let's keep in touch," he says to Ruth in a distracted way as he gets into his car.

He gets in touch sooner than Ruth expects. The phone wakes her at seven o'clock the following morning. In her sleepy state she hears David's voice crackling with anger or excitement, she cannot be sure which.

"Ruth! Have you seen the *Sunday Times*? You haven't seen anything yet? Sorry I woke you. Look on page five. I told you they wouldn't wait for our body to get cold. They must have had their meeting straight after the wake. Membership open to all African persons – and believe me, they don't mean white Africans – who write. Mogorosi is Chairman, Vusi Secretary, and Simon treasurer, and there's a glittering array of old friends on the committee. Let's meet for coffee before I leave for Lettland."

"'In my beginning is my end,'" she mumbles into the mouthpiece. "'In succession/Houses rise and fall, crumble, are extended...' David, I'll be in touch when I wake from the nightmare."

FIFTEEN

Amol iz geven ... once upon a time ... Magic words that suspend time...

So, Zalman, these days you want to suspend time, not spend it. What's changed? Remember what you wrote on the first page of your first black book, a mere three years ago? Turn back the pages, remind yourself. "...The present? That's why I'm writing, to use it up."

I've been dragged back into the turmoil of life by my shirt tails. And if there's one thing I've learned in my long and useless existence, it is that where there's life there's pain. My own I've learned to handle; the pain of others confuses me. I, the man with the remarkable memory, have forgotten how to ease pain. Once I knew. I would put my arm around Leibala, my younger brother, when his Cheder teacher beat him or when he fell out of the apple tree, and say, shah, shah, don't cry, it will pass, everything passes, the good and the bad. He believed me. Everything did pass, mainly the good. It's what happens while it passes that is so painful, so hard to bear. Like gallstones. No.

I am not yet ready to write about Leibala, the little lion. If only Michael didn't remind me so much of him...

So, Lola, the world is eagerly awaiting my memoirs. Let us not keep them in suspense. I shut my eyes and I'm a small boy again. It is Hanukah, the Festival of Lights, which, like Christmas, falls in mid-winter in the northern hemisphere, when the days are short and grey and the nights are black and endless, a wise time to bring light into people's lives. Outside the snow lies thick and white on the ground, indoors it is warm and cosy. There is a smell of freshly baked bread in the house, and of blintzes sprinkled with cinnamon and sugar. My mother has lit the eighth candle in this Festival of Light, and is waiting for my father and her six children to return from shul. We too are eight glowing sources of light and shall remain so until they begin snuffing us out. We are crunching through the snow, eager for the feast that awaits us, and my father is tarraraming a Yiddish song into his great black beard which is flecked with snow and his first grey hairs. He will not live to have a grey beard. The First World War is due to break out in seven years' time, and he will die of typhus in one of the cattle trucks that will transport the Jews deep into the interior of Russia...

No, Lola, I do not err; I am speaking about World War I. I am not ready to write of World War II. Perhaps I never will be. Cattle trucks are a favoured form of transport for Jews, be it into exile or to the gas chambers. No more interruptions; let me get on with my story. Jews are traitors, the Czar says; they will betray us to the Germans. So we are given twenty-four hours to pack a few things and leave house and home – the only home I've ever known – to which many will not return. And those who do will find roofs caved in, doors torn out, windows smashed, floors ripped up and furniture chopped up for firewood. No house is safe when its inhabitants are driven into exile. But, as yet, my father knows nothing of this, so he sings:

Hanukah, Hanukah, a yomtiff a greissen,
a lustigen a freilichen, nisht do noch a zanem...

126

It is so. Hanukah is a great festival, a happy one, when god, for a change, did something good for his chosen victims. In his abundant mercy, we are told, he delivered the strong into the hands of the weak and the many into the hands of the few. But not before thousands were slaughtered and the country lay in ruins. On the 25th day of Kislev in the year 168 BCE, Antiochus Epiphanes, who ruled the Syrian part of Alexander the Great's divided empire which included Palestine, very foolishly sacrificed swine flesh on the holy altar of the Temple in Jerusalem. The Jews rebelled. Under the leadership of the priest Mattathias the Hasmonean and his five sons, they took on the might of Antiochus' army – never underestimate the wrath of zealots and guerillas, you modern tyrants – and exactly three years later Judas Maccabeus, son of Mattathias, and his warriors entered the Holy City, purged the Temple of all idols, and rededicated it to Jehovah. Only one cruse of undefiled oil remained, enough to keep the Menorah alight for one day, but that miraculous little jug of oil lasted for eight days. Hence Hanukah, the Festival of Light.

But why, I ask myself, am I writing about Hanukah when it is Pesach? Perhaps because both festivals celebrate freedom, the first from religious persecution, the second from slavery. Or perhaps because Michael reminds me of Leibala who reminds me of Judas Maccabeus. In his acts, it is written of Judas Maccabeus, he was like a lion. He fought for an idea and died for it. May Michael live to 120 and die in his own bed. That's the nearest I can get to prayer.

The Jews battled against Antiochus and his successors for twenty-five years and all but one of Mattathias' sons were slain. Eventually they prevailed over the Seleucids, the second Kingdom of Judah was established, and there was, as they say in the Bible, jubilation in the land. The Kingdom lasted for seventy-six years, a blink of the eye in History, before it was torn apart by rivalries, murders, fratricides and matricides. In the year 63 BCE Pompey marched in, renamed it Judea, and that was the end of yet another revolution, not to speak of all the young men who died for it.

127

I read what I have written and again I marvel at my memory. Am I blessed or am I cursed? Not only do I recall useless details of my overlong life; I remember much that I have read. Most inmates in the Home are either forgetting names, dates and when to go to the toilet, or they have already lost their memory entirely. To me, that is to lose life itself.

Suddenly I become angry, very angry, with myself. Who do I think I am – god? What overweening pride tempts me to range over history so freely, so selectively, that I become smart with hindsight and shed alarm, pessimism and despair with every word I write? This pride – the Greeks have a word for it – has been my downfall. That is why I never made anything of my life: nothing seemed worthwhile. Everything, I concluded long ago, ends in fire and destruction, and leaves one with a taste of ash, if not in ashes. What's so important about survival if there's no hope, no joy? And what, I answered myself, is the good of joy if it leads to death? What's the point of living if you're going to die?

There are times when I hate myself so much, that I don't seek release in death. I have an obligation: after Leibala died I sentenced myself to life – and to remember.

The Next Day. I didn't sleep all night. It is always so when I become too angry, too excited. While walking in the grounds of the Home next morning, I bumped into Mr Sibiya who had just come to work. "Trouble, Mr Sibiya?" I asked, because he who always walks so tall and straight, had his head on his chest. When he lifted it, his eyes were clouded and his brow creased. I do not expect him to open his heart to me. He has seldom spoken about himself, except once when he told me how his family had been banished from their ancestral land and had come to live in Alexandra township. To my surprise, therefore, he said, "Too much trouble in the township. The children don't go to school. They say release the student leaders, give us books, give us proper education. Meantime they are not getting any education. They can't kill the government, so they kill each other. Even in my family there is trouble. Masilo, the youngest,

128

doesn't come home because he is fighting with Agnes. She doesn't come home because she is living with the policeman. My wife is sick and I am worried. It is bad, very bad."

If I had put my arm around him and said, "Shah, shah, don't grieve, Mr Sibiya," he might have thought I was completely off my head and felt obliged to report my lunacy to the Director. So instead I said, Mr Sibiya, let us forget our troubles and try our luck at Fah Fee this afternoon. Did you have any interesting dreams last night? When he looked at me, I saw the shadow of nightmares in his eyes. He shook his head, excused himself and went off to work.

Fah Fee fascinates me, Lola. Because you're a gambler, you will reply. Perhaps. But also because I once dabbled in Cabbalah. I'm intrigued by numbers, by symbols. No comparison, of course. Cabbalah has a loftier ideal than choosing a winning number in a game of chance with a Chinese man. It purports to be a philosophical system that was designed to answer man's (*and* woman's, my dear Lola) eternal questions on the nature of god and the universe and the ultimate destiny of man, that is, humankind. I gave up on the big questions a long time ago.

But I'm sure there is more to Fah Fee than a mere game or lottery. Do you know anything about it, Lola? Only what you've seen on the surface: black people gathering in the suburbs at certain times in certain places, and an elusive China, as they call him, who takes bets on a number he has 'pulled', pays out the winners, then drives off before the police pounce.

Mr Sibiya has explained Fah Fee to me many times, but I still don't understand. There are thirty-six numbers, each of which has an analogue. Thirty-five, for example, is dead man, and is paired with four, which is hole or big bath. Thirty-one is fire, and eighteen is small change. Thirty-six is stick or policeman with gun, which is paired with one, King. And so on. Mr Sibiya, I said once, I had a dream about a dead man. That is thirty-five, he tells me. But, I say, the dead man was riding a horse. Horse, Mr Sibiya says, is twenty-three. And in the background a great fire is burning. Fire, he tells me, is thirty-one. So what number must I back? I ask. From the look on Mr

Sibiya's face I realise that I've missed the point somewhere. The names of the numbers are strange to me: diamond lady, skelm, little water, dead man, and, you'll pardon me, shit, amongst others. As I said, it could be just a game of chance. On the other hand, it may have more mysterious origins which might never reveal themselves to me.

A few months ago I plotted to take over the Fah Fee run from the China who services the Home, to relieve the tedium of daily life if nothing more. Far more exhilarating than occupational therapy, you must agree. No, you won't agree. Neither did Mr Sibiya. He advised me strongly against it. They will win all your money, he said. That won't take long, I said. What he actually meant was, you don't understand the people, their dreams or the magic of numbers, but he's too much of a gentleman to say so.

Then I had another idea: I'd adapt Fah Fee to Cabbalah and start an ethnic game among the white residents of the Home: Aleph, for example, represents the number one, an ox, plus everything that exists and doesn't exist. Bet, number two, is the symbol of all habitations (like houses and Homes), and so on. I'd have enjoyed working out such a system. The thought of having to use it among this depressed community, however, put me off; their dreams can only be of death, if they dream at all.

I'm not a social worker, Lola. I don't have your limitless compassion and patience. I'm short-tempered and irritable. All this stuff I've written about easing the pain of others is sheer bluff. I have tried before, in these little black books, to ennoble myself. Mostly I catch myself out.

Yes, I would have liked to be a China to the blacks; they are so easily moved to joy, to singing and to dancing. And how stoic they are in sorrow. I'd gladly have lost my entire fortune for the pleasure of watching them win. Despite Mr Sibiya's reservations, I think I understand what underlies their addiction to this game. It gives them an outlet for their dreams. It also allows a little hope, a respite, between the dream and the reality.

Naturally, I'd have been expelled from the Home. For me that would have been a welcome release; for you, dear Lola, it would have meant humiliation and worry. Michael would have taken me in, I'm sure, but there is always the question of T-shirts. Unless you have a T-shirt with a message for the world, you can't live in Crown Mines. Forgive me, Michael, I jest. I take you very seriously. Hence my gloom.

After Mr Sibiya went off to work, I sat down under this tree, my little black book on my knee, ready to continue where I left off last night. Mr Sibiya, even his darkest moods, has a calming effect on me.

A few nights ago we celebrated the first Seder at your house. Celebrated? Well. There was you, Paul, Michael and me, and, of course, Chantal's in-laws. They have recently returned from a visit to Australia where Chantal, her husband and their two young children live. (Why do I tell you this, Lola? You were there. Do I write these memoirs for you or do I harbour other ambitions? Who knows what goes on in the minds of old men.) Chantal's father-in-law, Oscar, is rich and pompous, has pulp in his cranium and a stone for a heart. He believes that his fortune, acquired in the manufacture of ladies' underwear, has made him an expert on everything, including Jewish history and tradition. In fact, he acquired his erudition not by study but by osmosis; by going to shul every Friday night. Saturday morning he goes to the office.

I turned down the honour of reading the Haggadah, so Oscar did it, ponderously, with an old-world Ashkenazi accent, relishing the sound of his own voice. Michael sat next to me, crumbling a piece of matzo, looking very tense and unhappy. He is the only truly joyous person I know and when I see him like this, I am disturbed. He has had a serious argument with you about a girl he is living with. He wants to talk to me about it. He also wants me to meet her. With pleasure, I told him. We've arranged he'll bring her to the Home next week.

In the meantime, Oscar bumbled on, blessing the lord, the matzo, the wine and everything else in sight. Michael does not like Oscar. He once kicked him out of his factory after he had got permission to address the workers. Oscar has a bad name in trade union circles. I think Michael feels about him as I do about that rogue Silverman who used prison labour to slave on his potato farm. But he sat quietly as Oscar muttered and spluttered, until Oscar said in a very patronising manner, "Well, Michael, as you are the youngest, you may ask the Four Questions."

I heard something explode in Michael.

"Right," he said, as he stood up. I've heard him ask the four questions before; he knows them by heart: Why is this night different from all other nights, and so on. But this time he had a different set of questions.

"Why," he began, "when we ourselves have eaten the bread of affliction, do we not share our bread in this land of plenty and starvation, with those who have laboured to produce it?"

There was a look of alarm on your face, Lola. You made warning sounds deep in your throat but Michael ignored them.

"And why," he went on "when we ourselves were slaves to Pharaoh – Avadim hayinu l'pharoah b'Mitzraim," he read out of the Haggadah – "do we permit others to be slaves to us?"

By this time, Paul, who was sitting at the head of table looking very bored indeed, sat up straight.

"And how can we, who know what it is to be strangers in strange lands, keep silent while people are wrenched from their ancestral land at the whim of the powerful, and exiled to foreign places?"

Only then did Oscar, who had been smiling benignly, catch on. His face grew redder and redder and he might have stormed out, had he not been so fond of your kneidlach.

"And how can we," Michael concluded, "for whom justice is the pivot of our traditions, stand by and watch in silence the persecution and oppression of another people?"

He said all this quickly, clearly, then got up and left the house. I heard his motor cycle start up and roar away. I cannot begin to describe the shock on everyone's faces. Oscar mumbled something about the young who didn't understand, his wife Esther fiddled with her diamond rings and wiped the perspiration from her upper lip, and you, your face on fire, apologised profusely and explained that Michael had had a stressful time of late. Paul, as usual, said very little, but he no longer looked bored. I suspect he was rather proud of Michael.

Oscar got on with the reading of the Haggadah, twice as fast as he would normally have done, putting special emphasis on Rabbi Elazar's commentary on the meaning of Pesach. "The *Torah* says in four different places, that a man should tell his son the story of how we left Egypt. The reason is that the *Torah* wants to explain the way to answer four different kinds of sons, one wise, one wicked, one simple and one too young to know how to ask questions…" Oscar slowed down and read the part about the wicked son with great emphasis. What the idiot doesn't realise is that Michael understands the real meaning of Passover better than all the sons rolled together.

Oh, Michael, Michael. My heart aches for you.

SIXTEEN

3 October 1983
...You ask why I've stopped sending the prison letters, Jeanne.
I don't do the correspondence any longer; I've too many other
commitments. Mary, my ex-mentor, now works four days a
week at the Advice Office and does the correspondence at
home. I'll ask her for copies of some letters and send them on
to you. From what she tells me, the letters are much the same.
She also pesters the lawyers, but they are busy with political
detainees. "Let's face it," the lawyers used to say to me,
"you're talking about hardened criminals. If they broke into
your house, they wouldn't hesitate to shoot you." They're
probably right, but I am haunted by those letters. These
'criminals' are human beings; they are suffering. Their
sentence is to be removed from society and imprisoned, not to
be abused by the sadistic warders and gangs who run the jails.

I go to the office quite often; to plan protest vigils, to co-
ordinate our activities with other women's organisations and
so on. We meet in the chapel downstairs, the safest place in
the building: we've combed it for bugs. Michael used to insist
we have spies among us; I disagree. I don't have many talents,

135

but I pride myself on being a discerning judge of character. I know these women, and there isn't a spy among them. Besides, what is there to be afraid of? We work within the law. The black women in our group are very conscientious, particularly Agnes, a most intelligent and beautiful young woman from Alexandra township, with a glowing black skin, shining white teeth, and nails painted brilliant red. She often comes to the house where we prepare the agenda for the next meeting. She always asks after you, Chantal and Michael. When I told her you were doing well with your dancing, she looked wistful; she has always wanted to be a dancer. Chantal and her family are settling in well in Australia and Michael is in London, studying. That's all I've said about you. All her siblings, she tells me, are in exile. She doesn't say much about them either. And even less about her family, who live in Alexandra township. I've often given her a lift home, but don't know if it's to the home of her parents, friends or lover.

Each time I walk into the foyer of the Advice Office, the sad-eyed Christ-on-Tapestry puts on his 'wherefore hast thou forsaken Us?' mien, but I look him straight in the eye and say, "I haven't gone AWOL; I've only moved to another department." There's much to protest about. Contemporary history is written on our placards: TROOPS OUT OF THE TOWNSHIPS; SADF: HANDS OFF OUR NEIGHBOURING STATES; END CONSCRIPTION; RELEASE THE CHILDREN, to name but a few of the issues in which I'm personally involved.

The Advice Office, as always, is crowded, with queues backing into the vestibule. I have a sinking feeling that even after the Struggle is over and the Resurrection or Reconstruction or Reformation has begun, the queues will still be there, and letters will still be coming in to ask for 'an intercede' from our 'Honourable Bodies'.

I'm kept so busy I don't have time to think about Michael. When I remember the decline I went into after he left the country, I feel ashamed. I should have been happy that he was leaving this hell-hole and that he was temporarily removed from his obsession with you-know-who, but I was filled with dread and anxiety. I didn't get to see him before he left the country, but Zalman told me he was a changed person when he came out of detention. Fifty-eight days in solitary, regular interrogations, and they could find nothing to charge him with. Next time, he told Zalman, they'll have plenty ... No, I cannot bear to think of it. We've had one postcard from him so far, postmarked London, of Princess Di shaking hands with a leper. Strange choice. Don't be surprised that he hasn't contacted you. Zalman pointed out that it took two months from the time Michael dated it, for the postcard to arrive. He's probably moved on ... Let's get back to the general situation.

I feel very despondent when black anger doesn't find its true target and communities turn upon themselves. What hope have they against the Hippos, the Casspirs, the helicopters and the guns? Black councillors and other 'sell-outs' suspected of collaborating with the authorities, get instant justice: necklacing. You've heard of it. A car tyre is slung around the neck of the condemned, his/her hands and feet are tightly bound with cord, the tyre is doused with petrol, then set alight. I can't look at a tyre without a chill of horror. Shops, council offices and beerhalls are burned down; petrol bombs are thrown into 'traitor's' homes. But the main violence, of course, comes from the army and the police who have become a constant presence in the townships. They haven't brought law and order to the townships, only death.

Now that the violence is spilling over into the white suburbs, there's a growing awareness of the black townships, far out on the outskirts of towns: Sebokeng, Boipatong, Ilingelihle, Tumahole, Bhongolethu, Galeshewe – who had ever heard of them before? Today they are occupied territory. Soldiers and police patrol the dusty, rutted roads and roadblocks seal them off from the white areas. When Michael used to say we were in the midst of a civil war, we thought he was exaggerating. Soldiers and police shoot anyone who lifts a stone or moves too fast or unexpectedly. I've seen them, these Angels of Death: young conscripts with short hair, sitting on top of their monstrous armoured cars, holding guns in their shaking hands. But make no mistake: there are trigger-happy brutes among them who are out to get the 'terrorists'. And get them they do.

I've been to many funerals lately, most of them the result of police violence. We go as representatives of the organisation, to give solace to the grieving mothers. Last week the son of one of the Advice Office interpreters, Sophie, was shot, together with three other youngsters who had thrown stones at Casspirs which had blocked off the road to the cemetery during a funeral. These are not funerals, the police say; they are illegal political gatherings. To protest against illegal political killings, one might add.

Sophie is a widow and had two children. Her older daughter has been in exile since the 1976 uprising. We found Sophie sitting on the floor of the front room of her tiny house, surrounded by members of her extended family, dressed in black garments, receiving crowds of neighbours, friends and strangers, who filed past endlessly, saying words of condolence. She is obviously devastated by the death of her only son, but she was stoic and dignified. Such courage. One can see where she gets her strength from: there is a wonderful sense of solidarity in the townships.

As we were leaving Sophie's house, a nephew of hers invited us to join him at the soccer stadium; something special was about to happen, he said. When we hesitated, he told us not to worry, it was safe to go. The residents had prevailed on the Minister of Police to keep the Casspirs out of the township that night so they could mourn in peace; they themselves would keep good order.

There were four of us: Mary, Dorothy and Edna from the Advice Office, and myself. On our way to the soccer stadium, we were swept into a stream of comrades who were dancing down 10th Avenue, singing freedom songs and chanting, "Oliver Tambo is our Father. Viva, Oliver!", "Viva Mandela!" which were answered with vigorous hai! hai! hai's! from the crowd. I was separated from the other women and Sophie's nephew, and became part of the crowd. I found myself between two young men who linked arms with me and said, "Look, Mamma, like this," showing me how to toyi-toyi. It was one of the most moving moments of my life. I was practically lifted off my feet as I got into the rhythm of the dance, or trot, moving from one leg to the other, and chanting, at the top of my voice, "Viva Oliver Tambo!" "Viva Mandela!" in this marvellous choir of voices that rang through the warm night. I cannot describe how exhilarating it was to feel, even for a short while, part of this surging, vital, crowd. I also understood, for the first time, the look of ecstasy I'd seen on the faces of protesters as they sing and dance in the face of armed soldiers and police.

Across the valley, lights of the white suburbs mapped out another country, a strange, introverted country which is unaware of what is happening on its own borders. A full moon rose over the Jukskei as the speeches began, lighting up the green, black and gold flags and banners of the ANC. An anonymous member of Umkhonto we Sizwe, who had spent many years on Robben Island, spoke from the rooftop of a bakkie, in the middle of the stadium. He had a voice like an injured lion. "We are facing a very strong enemy," he roared, "and you will only win the struggle if you are disciplined and united..." The crowd responded with cries of "Viva!" "Bopha!" (unite) and something that sounded like Boo-ah, which, I was told by a black lady wearing the red-lined blue cape of the Sacred Heart Church, means "speak!" said in affirmation, like amen. A poet in flowing robes chanted verses, and women ululated.

Another speaker said he stood before his people with tears rolling at the bottom of his heart for the dead comrades who had done the rightful thing, but others would take their place ... No, Jeanne, I'm not mocking the language; tears are rolling at the bottom of my heart as I write this. Like the letters that pour into the Advice Office, the speech of the people is a condemnation of a system that has kept them down, denying them all rights, including that of education.

Groups of comrades, some dressed as guerrillas in brown

coveralls, kept order in a quiet, efficient way. At one stage two informers were caught with tapes in their bags and hundreds of people rushed at them. The young marshalls restored order and the informers were warned and released. How they will continue to live in their community after this is another matter.

When there are no police present, Sophie's nephew told us when we eventually found one another, there is no violence.

It is strange. When I drive into the garage at night after a meeting, I look around nervously before I get out of the car. In this crowd of about 20,000 people, I felt safe, protected, part of a greater community. How sad that it can only be a momentary experience. I would gladly strip myself of everything and go to live in the townships, if I could become a real part of it. So why don't you? you may ask. Because it seems I have a different history, a different destiny. But I shall never leave this country; I love it and its people. This is where I belong.

We've been through some turbulent years since you left, Jeanne: school boycotts, refusal to pay rents, stay-aways, street committees, people's courts, killings, burnings, shootings. In spite of the upheaval, however, the townships have not become ungovernable as Pretoria claims. I myself saw a radiant example of it that night, but this is the exception. The policy of divide and rule persists, and it works. Even white school children are being indoctrinated. Watch the servants in your backyards, they are told, and report any suspicious goings-on. Remember, the tame dog is the one that bites hardest.

So the atmosphere is thick with fear and distrust. As soon as any leader appears who speaks of living together in peace, he or she is locked up or disappears, and chaos descends again.

I try to understand the desperation and rage which underlie some of the terrible events that take place in the townships, but I cannot: our lives have been so safe, so protected. And, in spite of a few luminous experiences, I can't shake off this feeling of impending upheaval and doom. And I feel utterly helpless in the face of it...

Love, Ma.

P. S. Mary has given me copies of some of the letters she's received lately. As I read through them, I remembered my feeling of helplessness and desperation when I handled the correspondence. Who knows what goes on behind those high prison walls, real and metaphorical?

Right Honourable Sir,
With my decorous manner and with my respect of law and regulation especially under prison law and treatment of prisoners, I respectfully submitt that, on June 21, I comitted an escape which were never succeeded through ...
Furthermore we all six (6) prisoners will appear in Randburg C Court in November. We are highly assaulted by authorities and isolationed since June month. Honourable sir our attention is to get a defendent in such case. May you please keep on touch before or on date of court...

Please have clemency, Justice reconsalation on ours and consider.

Your obedient convict,

Dear advisser,
This letter is optinist about my recertive to you. I know you are utilitarian about this exclude of this prison reckless,, Me, I cant tell my name and numbers because they will kill me,, Onces they know I writte a letter to you I will lost my life,,

Our parence they did know about this,, because we tell them at our visite time,, Please can you take my eridite to the newspaper please,,

First we did get prison rights and all our rights they take for their self,,

Second our ration food we did get as is fateful,, and prison offices take our ration to they houses,, and medicine ... They come to you at midnight at single cell and kill you,, because no one see them at night,,

141

All this I write here is factual of this prison,,
My exponent is extremity,, All is otpinist,,
Third. The district surgeon of this prison,, has not do his redeem to sick prisonners,, He allway reckless way to prisonners,, One day I hear him say to other prisonner,, I will let you go to your parence with a tikert on your feet,, because you are complaining about your sicknnes,,

Now how will we do about all this reckless always redound to us prisoners of doing our sentence from the law forensic euphemism...

Sir,
This letter is indictment and indestructible Please I need a intercede...

Office, I great you with optimist. I have no parental and I serve a long term inside prison at Maximum and I haven got money I am penerious. I have a ordeal here at maximum about oraculuar to me. I was assaulted often here inside prison about prohibitive of preservation.

Epistle. I am inert about prison official here inside prison ... Inside prison courts the difine of prison officials coercion about the assault against me because I lack of lament and legal attorney. They are laborious lawless codifying and deceiving me because I am a prisoner of defectiveness and larceny and I am negetive to them about their obligatory and they negative to me and negligible about the obvious assault on me and they obliterate my complain of assault. I need a physician to examine my physique about my assault. Because I have perdition of malancholia from the day I was assaulted and I was given a pain physic from prison district surgeon ... Now I inundate your interview at Leeukop Maximum service as agent. Please help me with proficient. And I probity your organisation.
Thank you

What does he thank us for? We can't help him with 'proficient' and he 'probities' our organisation in vain.
Love, Ma.

SEVENTEEN

Where have all the years gone, I ask the wrinkled, hollow-cheeked image that stares back at me from the mirror. Into your little black notebooks, he answers with an arrogance age has not dimmed. Everything he knows. Four notebooks in six years. I write only when I must. If everyone wrote only when compelled to, and if those with "half a mind to write" desisted – who needs the scribblings of half-wits? – fewer trees would be felled and our earth might become a better place, if one is to believe a new breed of do-gooders who have crawled out of the compost. Greenies, they call themselves. I didn't like being called a 'griener' when I arrived steerage from Lithuania to South Africa. Red I would have tolerated; it was almost obligatory to be red those days. Not green. But the times, says one of Michael's favourite singers – the one with adenoids – are a-changing. As I walk to the back of the Home every day to place my bet with the Fah Fee runner, I find myself mumbling, in perfect English, 'the times they are a-changing'. I miss Michael more than I can say, so I won't say it.

Write, you always urge me, write. So I write, despite my fears for the rain forests of Brazil. (I am not scoffing, Lola; I am concerned about our planet earth, though I'm not likely to become a griener, not at my age.) But where is it written that I should only deal with the past, the present and the future? Sometimes I try for the timeless: I make patterns and pictures with words. If I hadn't become so concerned about 'pollution' – how would one say that in Yiddish? Shmutz? – I'd write more. Who knows? Had I started earlier, I might have stood on the bookshelf next to the other Russians. As you see, I am my usual modest self. Everyone changes except me.

You, for example, have changed beyond recognition. You're thinner, prettier, even taller, (though I don't understand how that happened, unless I've grown shorter). But you've also become a woman of stature in another sense, at least in my eyes. After Michael was detained, I thought you would end up in the psychiatric clinic next door. You wept and you railed, then grew silent and withdrew into yourself. When you emerged, you were no longer the guilt-ridden do-gooder I've always known; you were a woman warrior. I've read about animals that kill to protect their young, but I've never known of a woman who takes on the entire armed forces of a country, from public platforms noch. Yes, Paul brought me to a meeting but made me promise not to tell you. Dead men, however, may tell tales.

"All our sons," you said in a strong, clear voice – I have the yellowing newspaper report stuck in my notebook – "black, white, and brown, are being drawn into a tragic conflict which cannot be resolved through violence but which has already claimed many young lives. Hundreds more are leaving the country because they refuse to serve in an army which is being used to enforce a deplorable system. Mothers," you said, "must reject their traditional role of passively accepting the blood-letting of our youth and demand an end to conscription. It is the inalienable right of the individual to follow the dictates of his conscience, and it is the privilege and duty of mothers to support such sons."

Michael would have been proud of you. To think I once advised him to shoot off a toe!

"Nachas from nieces," Paul had said as we slipped away after the meeting. "And from ex-wives," I said. "Don't grieve,

144

Zalman," he responded in his usual ironic way, "and don't worry about me. I'll survive. Our marriage was dead. It took Michael's detention then departure to shock her into realising it. She's stronger than you think. It's just that I'm getting sick of fried eggs. Lola has custody of Grace."

I was very worried about you. I thought you had been struck down with the hereditary madness Michael used to joke about. There you were, alone in that huge, echoing house, one daughter in Australia, another in Manchester, your son, goodness knows where, and what do you do? You kick Paul out. After all those years. Who's even talking about love? At least there's someone in the house to speak to, to take the dead cats off your front verandah, to help you change your slashed tyres, or to put out the fire from the petrol bomb. All this had to happen before you realised you were no longer living in a safe house. Michael used to scoff at your security arrangements: the electronic garage doors, the alarm, the iron grills over the windows, but those fascist lunatics managed to breech the lot. And they weren't only getting at you; they were also sending a message to Michael. And how did they know so much about you and your family? There are spies in your organisation, Lola. Paul and Michael always said so and I agree with them.

But thank goodness you moved into that very nice apartment, with a watchman at the front door, and buttons and radios and locks and peepholes. I miss the Sunday afternoons on your lawn, under the willow tree, with the young ones around the swimming pool, their hearts on their T-shirts ... Enough of that. If you can bear it, so can I.

But perhaps you are being too strong. You need to cry a little, sigh a little. When you are being so strong and active and decisive, you remind me a little of your mother. Only a little. She had no outlet for her powerful personality so she enmeshed her family in it. You, at least, have a cause. Perhaps I should buy you a little black book in which you can keep in touch with your more tender feelings, and say how much you miss Michael, how much you love him. I know he is your favourite child, though your relationship soured after he met Sara. I make no secret of it: Michael used to bring her to visit me and she still comes. She loves Michael very much.

You who have changed so much, Lola, change a little more; get to know Sara. She is uncertain of the future. She has graduated from medical school, completed her internship, and is now working at the Alexandra Health Clinic. But why do I tell you this? You know everything that goes on in the Singer household. Your Grace and their Selina are sisters and they spend hours talking to one another on the phone. I'm sure you don't scruple to get the news from Grace. Why do I not have the courage to say this to you directly? Because you would take it as a lack of loyalty; you need at least one person in your life who does not judge you.

Get to know her, Lola, I should be saying to you. Don't become like my silly neighbour in the Home who must be ninety if she's a day, and who still weeps because her mother loved her sister more than she loved her. Forget old wounds. Put aside your meshugashen about her family, and think of her as the young woman Michael loves. Perhaps that's what upsets you; you are too possessive of him.

You even resented him spending his last night in the city, perhaps in the country, in my room, though you knew no one would look for him in a Home for the Aged. You and Sara were being watched, yet you were angry that I had not phoned you. I don't have to tell you how dangerous that would have been. The Clinic was not much safer but I had no alternative. A few words and Sara understood; she had been expecting it. Within the hour a colleague of hers brought Michael's passport, clothes and money to the Home. She did not come; you still don't believe that, do you? I understand your distress, Lola. To part without saying goodbye is hard enough; to think a relative stranger is closer to him than you are, is even harder. True, you have known Michael longer than she has, but believe me, she suffers no less than you do.

I never told you what happened that night; you were too angry, too distressed. Michael had slipped into my room late in the evening, hoping he had thrown off his 'tail'. Such concepts;

a tail. I was shocked by his appearance. He was thin, haggard and exhausted. They had released him only because they thought he might lead them to his comrades. They would certainly detain him again, he said; he must leave before dawn. He bathed, lay down on my bed and within minutes fell into a restless sleep. I sat and watched him for a long time.

Then I went downstairs to see if the parcel from Sara had arrived. Sipho, the night watchman who is also the chief Fah Fee runner, was on his way upstairs with it. We are old friends, Sipho and I, not like me and Mr Sibiya, but friends. "I've had a terrible dream," I said, taking him by the arm and walking down the stairs with him. "I dreamed a very big fish was chasing me. I swam and swam" – I, who would sink to the bottom of the sea if I fell in – "but it caught up with me. He opened his jaws and spat out hundreds of eggs which immediately hatched into enormous fish. I woke before I was swallowed up alive," I said to Sipho, wiping my dry brow, "but now I'm feeling very hungry. Instead of being eaten by the fish, I want to eat the fish, or anything else for that matter," said I, whose appetite would put a flea to shame. Sipho nodded gravely. Any Fah Fee player will tell you that fish is number thirteen or seven, and that eggs can be either twenty three or ten. "Remember that for the game tomorrow, Mr Zalman," he advised, unlocking the kitchen door; "maybe it can be lucky for you." "I am lucky already," I said, putting bread, cheese, milk and fruit into a plastic bag; "I am lucky to have a friend who feeds the hungry." He looked a little puzzled; such a thin man with such an appetite.

Michael slept for three hours; I dozed in the chair; gifted as I am, sleep is not one of my talents. When he woke, he ate hungrily. The rest of the night we talked, softly, in the dark, catching a glimpse of one another's faces only when we turned towards the light shining in from the parking lot downstairs. He said very little about his time in detention, and when he did, it was in a strangulated voice, as though his head were covered with a wet sack. I did not press him; I could not have borne to hear of his agony, coward that I am. He spoke mainly about the struggle ahead and about his hopes for the future. I read parts of my notebooks to him. Secret code, he had called the Yiddish writing a few years before.

Several times I called him Leibala. "Tell me about Leibala," he said. "You speak of him with great pain." "He was an idealist, a brave, selfless man," I said, "and was reviled in his narrow-minded community. History was not on his side, but neither was it on the shtetl's. He tried to save them. He commandeered a car from the town in which he was stationed – in my dreams I see it as a horse – and sped to the shtetl. "The Nazis are coming; they have already overrun Shavel. Flee for your lives! Save yourselves!" he begged them. They called him the usual names: Agitator, Communist. "We know the Germans from the First World War; we speak the same language," they said. "They are not beasts like your Ivans. Bitteshon, dankeshon, they say. They will not harm us. Out of here, you agitator." Leibala wanted to take our mother, two brothers, a sister, and his pregnant wife with him. "You will cause panic," they said, threatening to kill him. "Take only your wife and go." He embraced the family and left ... You know their fate," I ended my story abruptly. Why burden him with such horror?

I was, in fact, unable to finish the story. Until the dream that haunts me every night is dreamed to the end, I shall not be able to put it into words, not in my diary, not even to Michael. Only when I can dream it to the end shall I myself be free to die.

But let me turn to other things. I told you: you have changed so much. So has Mr Sibiya. He still comes to work every day from his smouldering township, but he has withdrawn into himself. He must be going through a very difficult time. He greets me like an old friend, but keeps to himself. And not because I've involved him in any mischief, as you may suspect. The Director told you; I've 'settled down'. They leave me alone and I leave them alone. They don't give me occupational therapy, and I keep to the rules, most of them anyway. They know I play Fah Fee, but they look the other way. As long as I have my sight and as long as the library brings me the books I want, I'm all right. But I admit I get lonely; Mr Sibiya was the only person I could talk to. And since Silverman had a stroke, I haven't even got anyone to hate. Who can get excited about a sack of potatoes, no matter how rotten? He just lies there in his cot, growing smaller every day.

I've forgotten why I decided to write today. I always start off thinking there's something important I need to say, then get sidetracked, impatient and frustrated. Unlike Michael and his friends, I have no messages for the world. I'd never have become a great writer: I haven't enough zitsfleisch, which means I can't keep my backside on a chair for long enough to write more than a few pages at a time.

One thing is certain; I'll never be a threat either to the great Russians, or to the rainforests of Brazil.

EIGHTEEN

The hall fills rapidly. Lola averts her eyes from the back row where Paul is sitting, near the door. Twice he has brought Zalman who has made no mention of it. She wonders what Zalman thinks of her speeches, but he does not reveal himself, taking refuge, as usual, behind the mask of a bemused shtetl Jew. Paul, on the other hand, is predictable. He certainly sneers at her 'noble' sentiments. She does not understand why he comes to these protest meetings, especially as he is denied the pleasure of telling her, afterwards, what a fool she is making of herself in public. She will regard herself truly liberated only when she stops wishing for his good opinion.

There are four speakers this evening. As people file into the hall, Enid MacCarthy, the Chairperson, with whom Lola has stood on many silent vigils, seats them, in speaking order, behind a long table on the platform. The Reverend Gregory Simpson, an outspoken opponent of apartheid who is working among the youth of a township in the Western Transvaal, is placed between Sophia Rakgoale, a resident of Alexandra township, and Lola. Samson Magubane, an activist from the Eastern Cape, sits on her right. Why Violence? is the subject.

Each speaker is expected to give the view of the group he or she represents: the church, residents of the townships, black activists, and concerned whites. The moral issues revolving around the increased violence in the townships is a delicate subject, and she has found it difficult to prepare her talk. She wishes Paul were not in the audience, but is pleased he has not brought Zalman this time.

She worries about Zalman. Since Michael went away, he has withdrawn into himself. At the Home he speaks only to the black staff with whom he plays Fah Fee, a situation which the Director, with uncharacteristic understanding, has chosen to ignore. He has also become very frail. He eats very little, sleeps badly, and his arthritis must cause considerable pain, but he never complains. What can you expect at eighty-four, he says irritably; that I should become a long-distance runner? I've run enough in my life.

Sophia Rakgoale, the first speaker, tells of the residents' suffering in the continuing violence in the townships. "We are caught between police violence and township violence and are divided by fear and suspicion," she says. "We don't know who will throw the next fire bomb; a political opponent, the vigilantes who work for the police, or those who pose as comrades."

As Lola listens, she regrets having prepared such a theoretical case against violence. Twice a week she works at the Crisis Centre in a white suburb adjoining Alexandra township where parents come for help in tracing their missing children. The files in her cabinet have cellophane tabs for each case: Red for the dead; blue for the injured; yellow for those who are missing, and green, the majority, for children in detention. She should have used the material in her files instead of spending hours in the Reference Library reading Thoreau.

The Reverend Simpson, whose ministry is in one of the largest townships in the Western Transvaal, speaks about the effect of violence on children.

"About a quarter of the 20,000 people in detention are under eighteen," he says. "Most of the children I have spoken to see their violence as acts of justice, even of self-defence. They come to terms with it, believing they have been good soldiers. But this violence turns on itself; it blunts emotion, brutalises them. As the enemy becomes inaccessible, and indeed appears to be unassailable, a witch-hunting climate is easily created, and the violence is deflected into their own communities. With the growing numbers of uneducated, unemployed youths roaming around in the townships, the cycle of violence is reinforced."

He tells of a twelve-year-old boy who had been accused of arson to whom he had spoken after his release from detention. "He readily admitted that his group of comrades, called The Fourteen, had burned down houses of black policemen and informers. He had been detained, tortured, and held in a small cell with three adults and two other children. He said they had wrapped electrical wires around his little finger, his foot and his genitals, placed a sack over his head, then given him electrical shocks. I thought I was going to die, he said. He dreaded being taken in again. But the struggle must go on, he said. When I asked what he wanted to do when the struggle was over, he said, I want to be a lawyer. I want to defend the people against injustice..."

Lola shudders. She looks around the audience, avoiding the back row. He too must be thinking about Michael. In the second row from the front, she sees her protégé Agnes, diligently taking notes. Such a conscientious young woman. She herself had not thought to take notes of the figures which the Reverend Simpson is now giving. They will certainly come in useful when compiling a list of detained school children in the Western Transvaal. As she listens, she becomes increasingly concerned about her own speech. She does not feel qualified to speak about violence. From the safety of her suburban town house, what can she know of the agony in the townships?

She is being introduced. "... Mrs Lola Stern, who needs no introduction..." Applause. Lola gathers up her notes, puts on her glasses, takes a sip of water and begins her talk.

"War and violence," she says in her clear public-speaking voice, "are as old as mankind; the concept of peace is only as old as civilisation. And it is civilisation which has spawned the

153

pacifist conscience." She acknowledges her sources scrupulously. After fifteen minutes of a potted account of pacifist sentiments from different cultures, illustrated by quotes like, 'where armies are quartered, only briars and thorns will grow'; and 'he that takes up the sword will perish by the sword', she concludes with yet another quote, from Thoreau's essay, 'Civil Disobedience':

> If injustice is of such a nature that it requires you to be the agent of injustice to another ... then break the law. Under a government which imprisons any unjustly, the true place for a just man is also in prison...

"The time has come," she concludes, "to adopt non-violent means of disobeying immoral and repressive laws and to refuse to take up arms to defend a system which we believe is violent and oppressive."

The applause reassures her. Perhaps it is necessary to give her mainly white audience a broader perspective against which to view the unmitigated horror of the violence which is tearing the country apart. As she sits down, the black activist who has recently spent months in solitary confinement for organising successful consumer boycotts in the Eastern Cape, gives her a withering look.

"Pacifism, civil disobedience," he mutters angrily. "True place for a just man. Have you been to prison lately? Jesus Christ, man, which planet do you live on?"

Lola stares at him, astounded. Despite her reservations, she feels she has made a daring speech. It is, after all, a punishable offence under the State of Emergency, to advocate the breaking of laws.

"Last week," he turns to the audience, "I saw the police fire point-blank into the stomach of a school boy who was protesting against overcrowded classrooms, lack of reading material and under-educated teachers. I heard his cry of agony as he ran away, trying to stuff his intestine back into his stomach. The police caught him and threw him onto the back of their truck. I heard later that he had bled to death. He was the third son his mother had lost over the last few years."

He speaks without notes, without quotes. "People are dying out there. Every funeral spawns another twenty funerals. Police fire on mourners, and the graveyards are littered with the new dead. Hospitals are prisons. If you're shot, you're a marked criminal. To avoid going to hospital, our young people cut out one another's bullets from their buttocks, backs and thighs with razor blades. Babies die at the breast, from tear gas. Balaclava-clad police roam the streets, shooting, sjamboking, tear-gassing. And we have only our songs and our toyi-toyi to keep up our spirits, and only stones to defend ourselves with. But singing causes riots, the police say. So they shoot the singers..."

His speech is greeted with muted applause. How does one acknowledge such revelations? The audience is shamed and discomfited.

Lola is congratulated when she steps down from the platform. Her organisation wants to publish her speech in the next issue of their magazine. Still burning with humiliation, Lola assents. She looks at the back row; Paul has left. He would have approved of the black activist's censure. And Michael? She draws herself up: she will no longer play to her gallery of critics. It has taken her too long to become her own woman; she is responsible only to herself. She is aware of her limitations, she thinks as she walks towards Agnes whom she promised a lift home. For a brief, intoxicating moment two years ago, when she had toyi-toyi'd and chanted and been carried away in that great wave of protesting blacks in Alexandra, she had felt a real part of their struggle. It had been an illusion. All she can do is dig her heels in and continue to speak up against injustice and oppression in the only way she knows.

Agnes is unusually quiet on the way home, apologetic for bringing Lola out so late at night. "Please let me off at the main road," she says. "It is too dangerous to drive into the townships these days. It is better I should walk."

"Nonsense," Lola says, winding down her window as she approaches the road block. Ahead of her is a straggly line of African taxis, a horse and cart, a few battered private cars and a delivery van. Some are waved through after a cursory search;

others are side-lined for closer inspection. After a while, an armed policeman approaches. He shines his torch into the car, letting it rest on Agnes' face.

"What is your business in Alexandra?" he asks Lola. "Don't you know we've got trouble here?"

Lola answers in a voice her mother would have used: "I am bringing my maid home. She worked late tonight. I had guests for dinner."

"Why can't she sleep in the kitchen or in the kaffir room in the backyard? People like you make trouble for us. They got no business here. Then we got to rush around, saving them."

"From whom?" Lola asks imperiously.

"From them." He nods at Agnes.

"I never feel in danger from Them."

"Look lady. We've got enough headaches without you. I've warned you. You want to get necklaced? Go. Ever seen what they look like afterwards? Smell like braaivleis."

Lola ignores Agnes' gentle nudging. She will not be intimidated by these crude, callous brutes.

"Sorry," Agnes says as they drive into the township. "Better to let me off here. He is right. It is not safe."

Lola pats her hand reassuringly and drives on through the dark, pot-holed streets. She knows where Agnes lives; she has brought her home many times.

As they approach Agnes' house, a group of children emerges from the shadows.

"Isn't it late for children to be running around? I'm surprised their parents allow them out in such uncertain times."

Agnes laughs bitterly. "Allow them? They tell their parents what to do. There are no children in the townships. They go straight from the breast to the barricades. Look down the road. See that soil? They've probably been digging tank traps. Even the army doesn't come into this part of the township at night. Sometimes you can understand why the police claim they don't have any children in detention. You must go now. It's not safe..."

156

The children, none of whom looks over twelve, gather around the car, thumping the doors as Lola stops outside Agnes' house, chanting something Lola does not understand.

"Please go," Agnes urges Lola as she gets out of the car.

One of the bigger children runs down the road and returns with a tyre, which he places over the head of a smaller child. Prancing around her, he shouts, "Nicklas! Nicklas! Agnes mpiempie! Nicklas!" The other children take up the chant, pantomiming stone-throwing and the striking of matches.

"Haai, voetsek man!" Agnes shouts, lifting a stone from the ground. A string of invective flows from her mouth. The children run off, jeering. Shaken, Lola drives away. She is not sure what has upset her most: the disrespect the children have shown Agnes, her ugly language in response, or the necklace mime. She drives hurriedly through the township, relieved to reach the road block without further incident.

"You again," the policeman grumbles, waving her through.

The familiarity of her own world restores her confidence. Why should she be shocked by the games township children play? They merely mimic the behaviour of their elders. Games, after all, reflect the society children live in. German children, no doubt, had goose-stepped, heiled Hitler and beaten up Jews with yellow stars pinned to their sleeves. Khmer Rouge children did not even play games; they had participated in the killings. Why should she expect different behaviour from township children? They had seen too much violence. Did she expect them to play a cosy game of housey-housey? There are no cosy houses in the townships. Neither, according to Agnes, are there any children.

Only yesterday she had read an article in which the writer said that school children have become the guerillas of the eighties. Tear gas, beatings and detention provide a crash course in the political struggle. They learn practical science by making petrol bombs; street sociology by taunting armed soldiers, politics by distributing pamphlets and painting slogans, and geography by the location of escape routes and safe houses.

What right has she to stand up in public, in such times, and without humility make speeches about pacifism and civil disobedience? She can see why the black activist feels she lives on another planet.

8 May 1985

My dear Jeanne, I was not pleased with my speech last night. I should have had the humility to refrain from recommending passive resistance in the face of violence from the police and army in the townships. I shall, in future, refuse to speak unless I have a real contribution to make – and I can't imagine what that could be!

You say I never write about my personal life. When I used to, you complained I was involving you in a conflict of loyalties. However, now that Dad and I are settling into our separate lives, we have a civilised relationship. (Our divorce didn't worry Chantal that much. She wondered how we had stuck it out all those years!) It's ironic. Since we parted, I've become visible to Dad again. On the rare occasions when we see one another, he comments on my weight loss, my clothes, but never on my public speeches. He pretends he doesn't know about them, but I see him at meetings, sitting in the back row, near the door, ready for a quick getaway. I allow him his fiction. But we can't live together; we get on better apart. He sees other women. I am only too happy that I don't have to please anyone any longer, that I can be myself. I have friends, of both sexes, and we are bound only by our common interests. I rarely feel lonely though I do miss you children. I had to wait for this 'liberation' until I was fifty-four. (Zalman, with his usual tact, says I overdo it, that I remind him too often of his sister, my mother – whom he regarded as a grimalkin. But at least, he adds, Paul didn't have to die in order to liberate you!)

No, I do not hear often from your brother, and I understand the reason. It's usually a postcard, addressed to me care of Zalman. I write to an address in London, but he's obviously not living there. It takes weeks, sometimes months, before I get a reply. But all I need, these days, is the assurance that he is alive and well. There's much I have to block out in order to survive and remain sane.

And no, I don't see Sara Singer. Why should I?

As you know Dad's been a key figure in the negotiations between the emerging black mine workers' union, and the Chamber of Mines. To his credit he has supported the workers' demands. Which side are you on? one of his bosses asked him. On the side of industrial stability, he answered. Michael would have approved, but I have a feeling they'll be giving him a golden handshake soon.

We now share Grace's services. In the beginning she worked only for me. We've given her her pension, but she wants to carry on working. She lives at home in Soweto and works one day a week for each of us, ironing, cooking, dusting. I sometimes drive her home. Usually there's a roadblock, and they don't let me into the township – 'for your own safety'. Which reminds me: I had a rather upsetting experience last night. Remember, when you were kids you used to play housey-housey, doctor and patient (yes, I knew about that – children are curious about one another's private parts); and school-school. From time to time, you'd also organise a concert for the children in the neighbourhood. You were always the star turn, Chantal was usually the usherette/cashier, and Michael, the infant prodigy, strummed on his toy guitar. As I was saying, last night...

"Hello." Lola slips her letter to Jeanne into her file as Agnes comes quietly into the chapel. "You're early. The meeting is for three-thirty."

"Am I disturbing you?" Agnes asks.

"Not at all. It's peaceful here in the chapel, so I decided to write a letter."

"To Michael?"

The memory of Agnes' hail of invective still rings in Lola's ears. "No," she says quickly, "it's my fortnightly letter to Jeanne."

"How is Michael?"

"Well. Very well. Enjoying his studies in London, though he

does miss home. He's a good correspondent. Writes regularly. White looks so good against your dark velvety skin, Agnes. You're a dramatic dresser. And your nails are always so well-kept. Lovely shade of red. Look at mine. Bitten to the quick."

"Your lecture last night was very good," Agnes says.

"Thank you, but it wasn't really good. It shouldn't have been a lecture. It was too academic, too theoretical."

"No, it was good. Are you serious about making illegal demonstrations in the township?"

"Yes. We've been too circumspect about breaking the law. Our next protest must be made in the township, to show solidarity. But to succeed, it must take the police by surprise. We don't want to be stopped before we get into the township."

"Of course not. We must keep it secret. Even walls have ears."

She responds to Lola's quizzical looks with a guileless smile.

NINETEEN

It is mid-winter. The days are short and cold, the nights black and frosty. The sun is at its farthest point from the equator, and the earth seems to be hurtling into dark, everlasting night. Or so it seems to Ezekiel Mzwakhe Sibiya, who used to be called John by the Director, who could pronounce neither Ezekiel nor Mzwakhe. But Mr Sibiya, as he is now called, does not measure his days by the winter solstice. For him the year is divided into commemorative dates which were conceived in violence and which continue to spawn violence: March 21, May 1, June 16, September 3, to name just a few. In March Mr Sibiya retrieved a newspaper from the Director's wastepaper basket which reinforced his bleak view of the world. "Only the South African government," he read, "could commemorate the silver jubilee of the Sharpeville massacre by shooting dead more blacks."

This has become the pattern of life – and death – in the townships. Every protest, every funeral, generates more deaths: a brief warning, tear gas, then the shooting begins, and the roads run red with blood. After the carnage in kwaNobuhle last March, the fire brigade hosed down the streets, and ambulances removed the dead and the dying. An ambulance orderly, tending a black youth, was baited by a policeman. "That bliksem's not writhing with pain," he laughed, "he's breakdancing." The orderly, shocked by his callous attitude, told a newspaper reporter about it. He lost his job. The 'breakdancer' lost his life. Mr Sibiya read all about it in the newspaper. He had to ask his neighbour's son what a breakdancer is.

Mr Sibiya, the Director says to him most days, go home before dark. We know there's trouble in the township. So he hurries through the barricaded back streets where even the Casspirs and the Hippos will not venture, and walks at a measured pace, looking neither left nor right. He only feels safe when he bolts the door, puts on his old cardigan, and sits down to a meal with Maria, in silence. It is three years since Masilo left home. Nobody knows where he is. Agnes, soon afterwards, had a child and moved in with her policeman. Mr Sibiya never calls him 'Gugile', only 'the policeman'. Come home, Maria begged Agnes after the policeman's house was fire-bombed. It is safer for you if I don't, Agnes had answered. But she leaves her child with Maria when she goes to work.

Everyone except Maria seems to knows what 'work' Agnes does. Those that did not, learned a few weeks ago at a funeral service in the stadium, a forlorn sandy acre at the heart of the township. While waiting for the hearses, the usual placards were paraded through the crowds: RELEASE MANDELA; FORWARD TO PEOPLE'S POWER; THE PEOPLE SHALL GOVERN; THE PEOPLE'S SPIRIT WILL NOT BE BROKEN. One unauthorised poster read:

BUY PEOPLE'S SPIRITS AT LIQUOR TOWN
VODKA R6.49, GIN R6.19.

The comic relief was short-lived: WRAB POLICE OUT OF THE TOWNSHIP, another poster demanded; AWAY WITH GUGILE AND AGNES. Mr Sibiya lowered his head and made his way out of the crowd. A leaflet addressed to 'black soldier, black policeman' was thrust into his hand. 'Stop killing your own people. Brother, soldier, policeman. The people of South Africa are on the march to freedom. Join us now...'

When the silence between him and Maria becomes too oppressive, Mr Sibiya tells her about the Home. Mr Zalman is her favourite character; his exploits make her smile. "He picks at his lunch," Mr Sibiya says, "then hurries to the big tree where Sipho, the head runner, collects bets for the China. And such dreams he has: the moon catches fire, the seas dry out, forests die; many strange things go on in his head." "Fire," Maria interjects; "that's dangerous. Warn him against fire." Mr Sibiya nods. "Moon is nine, fire is eighteen, should I pull those numbers? Mr Zalman asks me. He knows all the names and numbers," Mr Sibiya explains, "because he has written down what I told him. It is your dream, I say, you must choose. My dreams, he answers, aren't worth a pipke tabak. He sometimes speaks the Yiddish to me but these words I haven't heard before. A pipke tabak? I ask. He laughs. My dreams, Mr Sibiya, aren't worth a pipeful of tobacco; they all go up in smoke. As you can see, he says, I seldom win. And when he does," Mr Sibiya continues, "he gives the money away, usually to one of the women. You like the ladies, neh, Mr Zalman? the others tease him. I like the ladies, he answers, because they look after their children. You gentlemen would buy beer for your Friday stokvel or gamble it away." "He is right," Maria nods approval; Mr Sibiya knows she does not include him among the sinners, "he is right."

Since Mr Zalman plays Fah Fee, he has learned a lot about black people. Mr Sibiya, however, is not as close to him as he used to be. He is, after all, a white man who has had an easy life and who has not really suffered. He would never understand the terrible things that are happening in the Dark City, and as that is the only thing on Mr Sibiya's mind these days, he has little to say to Mr Zalman.

As he enters the house on this particular evening, he has a sense of foreboding. Agnes has not yet fetched her child; the mealie meal is burning; unwashed dishes are stacked in the sink, and Maria, her pink shawl wound around her waist, flits around like a caged sparrow. She pushes the mealie meal to the side of the stove, changes the child's napkin, washes her hands, dishes up Mr Sibiya's supper, and keeps looking at the back door.

"Something has happened, Maria." Her hands tremble as she puts down his plate. "What is it?"

"Eat," she says, glancing again at the back door. "It will get cold."

She hovers about the table, starting nervously when the wind rattles the broken lavatory door in the backyard. She peeps through the window, draws the curtain, then sits down, wringing her hands under the table.

Mr Sibiya pushes his plate aside. "I will not eat another mouthful until you tell me what's wrong," he says firmly.

"Masilo is back," she whispers. She claps her hand to her mouth. Tears stream down her cheeks.

It takes a little while for Mr Sibiya's vision to clear. Maria is saying something he does not understand.

"Masilo, Agnes, what? Speak clearly!"

"Wait!" Maria goes to the front door, puts her ear against it, returns to the table. "He may come again, but they are watching. There will be trouble tonight. He says we must lock our doors and stay inside. He is trying to stop the trouble but it may be too late. And there are other troubles, our troubles. He sent me to warn Agnes. The comrades are looking for her. But she wasn't there. Masilo says she must run from the township, go home…"

"This is home."

"To the farms, to my auntie Dora. If they find her … Listen! Footsteps."

"It is the wind."

"Listen!"

"It is the lavatory door. I'll fix it on Sunday."

"Footsteps! Blow out the lamp."

She lifts the baby from the floor. The door opens and an icy wind blows into the kitchen. A dark figure stands silhouetted, briefly, against the starlit sky. The door shuts, and Masilo gropes his way to the table.

"Father," he says in a low voice.

Ezekiel Mzwakhe Sibiya reaches out and touches the coarse

cloth of Masilo's coat. Like blind Isaac when Jacob came to steal Esau's blessing. Has thou but one blessing? Esau had cried. So he gave him the blessing which sounded like a curse ... "And by thy sword shalt thou live..."

Great sobs well up in Mr Sibiya's chest, and because it is black as Isaac's blindness and dark as Esau's fate, he allows them to spill from his mouth.

"Masilo!" he cries, "Masilo!"

"Listen carefully, father." Masilo clasps his rough hands. "In the church there's a meeting. When it's over, they'll be waiting..."

"I can go, I can warn them..."

"It is too late, father. They didn't believe me. No one trusts anyone, and when they do, they are betrayed. But the others can be saved. Find Sammy, you remember him, my school friend, at the People's Court in 15th Street. Tell him they must not take arms from those who call themselves freedom fighters; the arms are booby-trapped. The askaris, the deserters, are working for the police. I must leave. They know I'm back. Father..." He holds him close for a few seconds, kisses Maria, and as he goes towards the door, there is a flurry of footsteps outside. He hesitates, then slips into the bedroom.

The door bursts open and Agnes stumbles in. "Hide me! Hide me!" she cries, and throws herself down on the floor, breathless.

The child whimpers in Maria's arms. Mr Sibiya takes his hat and coat. "Come, Agnes," he says. "They will find you here." He helps her up. "Give her your shawl, Maria, she is without a coat, she is shivering. We will go to the Home, through the side streets. Stay overnight with the cleaning women and go to Auntie Dora with the first bus."

Agnes takes the child from her mother. "Look after ... forget who his father..."

"Where is his father?" Mr Sibiya asks. "Why does he not protect you?"

"His father," Agnes lets out a moan that seems to tear its way through her body, "his father is, dead. His father is burning! Oh my God, oh my God, oh my God!"

"Come! We must hurry."

"Wait." Masilo comes out of the bedroom. "You mustn't go with her. If they catch you ... You cannot help her."

"Masilo! You are my brother! Tell them. Tell the comrades I went to the white women's meetings, to their houses. Tell them we planned marches, protests. I gave the police names, addresses, dates. But I said nothing about the comrades. I didn't tell about the comrades!"

"Because you didn't know, because they didn't trust you. And now they don't trust me. Sell-out! Spy!"

"I couldn't help it, Masilo! Gugile forced me. Only once, he said. He needed the money, for the house, for a car. So I went to the meetings, and then I was trapped. The police said they'd kill me if I stopped, the comrades said they'd kill me if I didn't..."

"You were paid?"

"Yes, yes!" Agnes weeps. "They paid me R1000 a month. Gugile, he took it all, he beat me ... And now the house is burning, the car is burning, he is burning! Save me, Masilo, save me!"

"You must get out of the township, now. Not you, father, I'll take her. The township is sealed off by police roadblocks. But there is a way, over the stream, through the cemetery."

"It's a trap! I'm not going!"

"Quiet!" Masilo shakes her roughly. "You will get us all killed."

Agnes backs away. "You will hand me over to the comrades. You always hated me. Father's favourite, you called me. Oh father, I'm so sorry, I'm so sorry..."

"I've got real enemies to hate. You're just an mpiempie, a sell-out. But you're also my parents' daughter. Come."

"No!" She grabs the shawl from Maria, wraps it around herself, and runs out of the back door, leaving it wide open.

"Let her go, father. She deserves what's coming."

"'He that is without sin among you, let him first cast a stone...'" Mr Sibiya says, pulling on his coat.

"Still the Bible, still the church," Masilo says bitterly. "God's deaf. He doesn't hear oppressed people. We have to look after ourselves. I'll catch up with her." He hugs Maria and leaves.

"Lock both doors, Maria. If the police come, say Masilo has been away three years. I'll knock twice, like this, when I return."

"They will kill you also. Don't go!"

"You must go back to school, I told Masilo when he made the boycott that time. To hell with their gutter education, he said. They teach us to be servants and them to be masters. Masilo was right, I was wrong. Now I must go."

Mr Sibiya brushes past Maria and walks into the dark night. The air is thick with coal smoke. Sulphurous fumes from the Modderfontein dynamite factory drift in on the east wind and blend with the smell of burning rubber and stagnant gulleys. Mr Sibiya wraps his scarf over his nose and mouth and stumbles blindly along a road pitted with potholes and piled with garbage. The wind tears through his coat and gnaws at his bones. He clenches his teeth as he passes the silent, shuttered houses, aware that eyes follow his every move. The whole township is holding its breath, waiting to explode. As he approaches the church, he sees a line of light under the door. He slips to the side of a house near the church, and presses himself against the wall, choking on his heart beats. He hears the purr of a vehicle, the clink of metal. He is too late.

A long time passes before four men emerge through the church door. They are caught in the flood of light which is beamed from an armoured car at the side of the church. Dazed by the sudden glare, they hesitate, draw back, but are pushed outside by armed men behind them.

"A trap! Run, comrades!"

As they burst through the church gate, Mr Sibiya sees soldiers kneeling on the armoured vehicle, poised to fire. The first comrade runs past Mr Sibiya, shouting, "Now! Throw them now!"

Closely followed by his three companions, the leader stops, takes something from his pocket and as he lifts his hand, there is a burst of fire and a deafening blast. As Mr Sibiya falls to the ground, he hears screams of pain and terror.

This is Hell. He opens his eyes slowly and looks up at the orange, smoke-filled sky. Hell fires. A thousand devils are whipping my body and I cannot move my arms, my legs. And where is that terrible weeping and wailing coming from? The condemned? I have sinned and they have sinned. We let evil grow among us and watered it with our sins, just like the preacher said. And now we shall burn forever and ever.

"They're all dead," a voice says in the darkness. "It's too dangerous to move them now. We'll come back in the morning."

Afrikaans. Mr Sibiya is not surprised they speak Afrikaans in hell. But if he's in hell, why does he feel so cold? He tries to move but falls back in pain.

"They're coming out of the houses!" a devil is saying. "Back to the Hippo, quick! There's too many of them. Listen to that screaming. They can wake up the dead. If you come any nearer, we'll shoot!" he yells as the cries and ululations draw closer. "And if you interfere with the bodies, we'll bomb all your houses. Voetsek, verdamde terroriste!"

If you call things by their right names, Mr Sibiya thinks before he fades out again, things will come right. Freedom fighters, not terrorists ...

And this must be an angel, he thinks as a young woman with yellow hair bends over him. She is dressed in white, the walls are white, the ceiling is white. But heaven cannot smell like hospital. He must get up. Today the Director wants to clear out old papers ... He falls back and slips in and out of consciousness. Sometimes the yellow-haired angel is in the room; at other times, the black sisters. They talk loudly, chase people from the room, dig needles into him, then speak in whispers.

"...found this morning ... all four dead ... from the students' organisation ... police chased away people ... the bodies in the street all night ... dogs started chewing ... collect corpses in the morning, tear-gassed the crowds ... Hayi ... the worst ... only this old man ... maybe from the house ... wee in the night. Hayi ... Police want to speak to old man but he's unconscious. Want to leave guard ... doctor chased them away ... will come back ... say the grenades were booby-trapped..."

Mr Sibiya tries to get up, and manages to pull himself over

168

onto his right elbow. The yellow-haired angel comes into the room.

"I must go…" he croaks.

"How does your head feel?" she asks.

"Very big, empty. But I can move my legs. How long…?'

"You were brought in this morning. It is now three in the afternoon."

"Must go. Please. Take me. Must give the message. Court, Fifteenth Street…" He is afraid to say too much but has no choice.

She looks at him carefully.

"Bring a wheelchair, please," she says to the black sister. "I must get him out of here before they return. Where do you live? Is there someone who can look after you? Good, good. Gloria! Take his other arm. Nothing's broken, you're concussed. You'll have to remain quietly in bed for a few days. I'll bring the car around."

"Not home," Mr Sibiya says as the doctor drives out of the Clinic grounds. "Please. I must give the message. Fifteenth street." She nods; she seems to understand. The bright sunshine blinds Mr Sibiya. He closes his eyes and leans back on the headrest.

"Here we are." She draws up in front of a corrugated iron shanty adjoining a brick house. There are two burned-out cars on the other side of the street. "Have you got a name of anyone you want to see?" she asks as she gets out of the car.

"Sammy," he whispers.

"It's locked. Hey, comrade!" she calls to a young boy who is watching them from behind the car wrecks. "The old man wants to see Sammy. Can you call him?"

The boy turns away without answering, and goes up a lane between two houses. She shrugs and gets into the car.

"They don't trust anyone, especially a white face. I don't blame them. My white coat and stethoscope used to be a pass-port to any place. No more. The Clinic's in bad odour since the police raided our offices and took away our files. We couldn't stop them. They can do anything they like under the Emergency regulations. Look. Someone's coming. He's opening the door.

Do you think you can make it?"

Mr Sibiya nods. She helps him out of the car and they walk slowly towards the open door of the iron shanty. It is bare except for a rickety table and a few chairs. On the wall are two motor car tyres painted red and white. This is the first time Mr Sibiya has been into a people's court.

"I'll wait for you in the car," the doctor says as Mr Sibiya is helped into a chair by Sammy.

"Masilo," Mr Sibiya begins and chokes up. "Masilo says..."

In a shakey voice, he delivers Masilo's message and tells him what he saw outside the church the previous evening.

"Too late to save the others," Sammy says. "They should've trusted Masilo. It's because of..." He stops abruptly.

Mr Sibiya suddenly remembers Agnes. His heart beats irregularly and he begins to cough. Sammy helps Mr Sibiya to the car.

"Don't speak to anyone," he says, "and don't tell the doctor your name."

"She didn't ask. She told me I shouldn't remain in the Clinic, that they'd be back."

"You don't know whom to trust. I wish they had trusted Masilo. Get better soon, malume."

The doctor is quiet on the way home; she has to concentrate on keeping the car out of the potholes. Mr Sibiya holds his head in his hands, suppressing a cry every time they drive over a bump.

"To the left," he instructs her, and as they turn the corner, he sees a crowd gathered outside his house. The men are standing around in little groups. The women are weeping. He takes a deep breath, fighting off the dark. He leans heavily against the doctor and his breath comes in irregular little rasps as they walk to the front door. Through a haze he sees Maria on the floor, rocking on her haunches, silent. A neighbour is sitting on a chair next to her, holding the child. When Mr Sibiya enters the room, Maria looks up at him and with a terrible cry holds up her charred pink shawl. Mr Sibiya's legs buckle and he falls out of the doctor's grasp as darkness enfolds him.

TWENTY

"Come quick to Seventh Avenue!" A woman in a blue overall and canvas shoes without laces, pushes through the crowd towards Sara as she bends down to lift the old man. "Maria will look after him. His daughter, she is burning! Come quick!"

She grabs Sara by the arm and steers her out of the door to the car. Sara fumbles with the key; her whole body is trembling. She has never seen a necklace victim; they go either to hospital or the morgue. She does not have her medical bag with her and knows she should call an ambulance, but this distraught woman is literally hijacking her and she feels incapable of making rational decisions.

"I am Anna," the woman says as she directs Sara along the pitted streets, taking short cuts through narrow alleyways. "The auntie of Agnes, the cousin of her mother Maria. The people say she is a bad girl but you can't know. If someone points a finger, you are finished. Hurry, hurry! They say she was caught in Seventh Avenue. Turn left. No! The police are at the end of that street. Right, right! Into Eighth Avenue!" Anna shouts. "Just listen. Shooting, shouting, fires. Everyone is mad. Why are they killing each other? The police kill the comrades, the comrades kill mpiempies, and the mpiempies are making trouble for

171

everyone. There they are! There they are! Too many people. Maybe one hundred. Yesus! They will kill us also if we try to stop them. We cannot help Agnes any more. Smell. Can you smell? It is too late. We must go back!"

Sara opens the window. A sweet, sickly aroma intermingles with the smell of singed hair and burning rubber. The crowd is silent now, and through the silence Sara hears a soft hacking sound, which is followed by a low moan, a terrible animal sound that tears right through her.

She pushes the door open, and ignoring Anna's plea to back away, she runs towards the crowd, shouting in a hoarse voice, "Leave her, you murderers! Leave her alone!"

The people on the fringes drift away; the others yield before her infuriated charge. She finds herself in a cleared circle, at the centre of which sits a badly burned, half-naked woman, a cloth covering her lower body. Her arms are raised in mute, useless protest, and she emits a long, low moan as she keels over, falling face down onto the gravel road.

"Oh-my-god, oh-my-god!" Sara weeps as she bends over her. Next to the woman lies a blood-stained garden rake and a smouldering car tyre painted red and white. She is badly blistered and her skin has peeled off like strips of plastic to reveal blotches of red flesh. Her nylon socks have burned into her flesh and blood gushes freely from the hack marks on her head. Her finger nails match the colour of her blood.

A low mutter rustles through the crowd, rising to high-pitched screams of "Kill! Kill! Burn!" as the crowd closes in on Sara. For the first time since she dashed out of her car, Sara is shocked into reality. Frozen, she rises with difficulty to her feet, her fury spent, unable to say anything except "Wait! Wait!" as she holds out a restraining arm to the advancing mob. For a while no one touches her. They throw phantom punches, make crude gestures, and shout, "Kill the white dog! Zinji! Kill! Boer!" Then they jostle her, pushing her from one side of the shrinking circle to the other, until she stumbles against the dying woman and falls down beside her, landing with her face beside her outstretched hand with its blood-red nails.

172

"Leave her! She is the doctor from the Clinic. She is helping our people! Leave her!" she hears Anna scream. The smell of burning flesh and rubber, blood and faeces, has made her nauseous. She turns away, retches dryly, then staggers to her feet, holding out her hands: they are covered with blood and sand. The ululating and shouting dies down as a siren is heard in the distance. The rumble of armoured cars shakes the ground.

"Police!" someone shouts, and the crowd stampedes into surrounding houses, over rickety fences, and disappears through the fetid alleys that lead off the street. Sara and Anna stand next to the smouldering woman, their arms around one another, weeping.

As the first armoured car rounds the corner, Sara wipes her hands on her white coat, dries her eyes, and takes a deep breath. She must be controlled before her rescuers. Rescuers. An irrepressible laugh rises from her chest. No hysteria. Breathe deeply, breathe deeply...

"Round them up! Search the houses!" a stocky officer shouts as he jumps off the Casspir.

"Not Anna!" Sara pulls her away from a policeman who has grabbed her by the shoulder. "She brought me here, to try to save the woman! Leave her!"

"I give orders around here, lady. I need witnesses," the officer says.

"I'm not a lady, I'm a doctor, from the Clinic! We came too late! We saw nothing! Please, release her. And the burned woman must go to hospital. I know. I'm a doctor!"

"Too late for doctors," he says as the ambulance screeches to a halt behind the Casspirs. A medical orderly steps out, turns the woman over with his foot, covers her with a blanket and motions the stretcher bearers to take her away. "To the morgue," he tells them.

"This woman is in shock," Sara says, keeping a firm hold on Anna; if she lets go, she herself will fall. She fights recurring waves of nausea. Mustn't faint, mustn't vomit. Firmness, strength. Can't give in now. "I must take her to the Clinic, for treatment, for shock."

The officer is distracted by a shout from one of the alleys. "Get the bastards!" he shouts, barging through the gate of a house. "Follow me!"

"Quick, before they return!" Sara whispers, pushing Anna towards the car. "The Casspirs haven't closed me in. Which way to the Clinic? I don't know where we are."

By the time they get back to the Clinic, Sara is shivering violently. The black sisters take charge of Anna and Sara is taken into the doctors' common room by her colleague Reggie. He helps her out of her blood-stained coat, gives her two pills and a glass of water, and helps her onto the couch, covering her with several blankets. He sits beside her, his hand on her shoulder, until she falls into a troubled sleep.

"Want to talk about it?" he asks when she wakes up.

She shakes her head. It is dark outside. She looks at her watch. Six-twenty. She must go home, wash the blood away. Which home? Not her mother's; she will panic. Crown Mines? Oh Michael, Michael; where are you? I want to go home to you. She begins to weep softly. She stands up unsteadily, then subsides onto the couch again.

"I'll drive you home," Reggie says. "Better still, come to my place. You shouldn't be alone. And don't come in tomorrow. I'll take your shift."

"Thanks, Reggie. I'm, all right, really." she says. She gulps down the sugared black tea which one of the nursing sisters has brought her, and holds out the cup for more. "I can drive. Just a little tired. I need sleep. I'll be fine by tomorrow. No need for double shifts. Enough work as it is."

She gets up, puts on a clean white coat, and walks slowly through the Clinic, keeping a tight grip on Reggie's arm.

"Renewed violence, as you no doubt saw," he says.

Medical orderlies and nurses are pushing trollies into the overcrowded theatre; doctors are putting up drips, swabbing, suturing, resuscitating people who have been shot. In a quiet corner stand two trollies with the sheets drawn over the entire body. There has been no time to remove the dead. As she walks along the corridor, she smells burning flesh.

174

"I can't," she says, her knees buckling. "The smell. Burning."

"You know what that is." Reggie takes a firmer hold on her. "Let's look in."

He pushes open the door of a makeshift theatre. A doctor is standing over an anaesthetised boy on a trolley, cauterising a leg vessel, which he holds in a metal forceps, with a diathermic needle.

"See? Stopping the bleeding."

"Of course," she says quietly. "I don't know what's got into me..."

"You shouldn't be driving," he says as he opens the car door. "Please, let me take you home."

"I'm okay." She smiles. "Just a little overwrought. Thanks, Reggie. See you tomorrow."

If only she can reach den safely, just this once, everything will be all right, she thinks as she approaches the road block. All she needs is a hot bath and a long sleep; she has been working long hours. She cannot crumple at the first threat to her personal safety; people in the townships experience this every day. She slows down. She usually approaches the road blocks with anxiety, especially if she is carrying an unrest victim in the car. Anyone shot by the police is deemed to have been guilty of wrong-doing. Helping the injured makes one an accessory to the 'crime'. She has been detained twice for refusing to answer questions to the satisfaction of the police. An armed policeman shines his torch on the seats and floor of her car and waves her through.

She has also had problems on the other side of the barricades. If she encounters comrades who recognise her from the Clinic or from meetings and funerals, she is given safe conduct to the Clinic, sometimes to the accompaniment of hearty viva's and energetic toyi-toyiing. But should she be stopped by the more aggressive, non-politicised gangs who are roaming the township, exploiting the chaos, they are likely to respond to her clenched fist – proffered with a degree of self-consciousness – by throwing stones, banging on the roof of her car or trying to overturn it. Her white coat and stethoscope have lost their magical properties; they no longer shield her from black bitterness. As she found out this afternoon.

"Don't answer back," Michael used to say, when she told him about her problems at road blocks; "save it for important things." "Strange advice from someone who spells out his defiance on his T-shirts," she would reply. "All discarded. If they want information, they'll have to prise it out of me." Which is what they probably did during those months of solitary confinement and interrogation. She had not even seen him before he left. "He is thin and pale," Zalman had told her, "but his spirit is strong."

In an earlier, more innocent age – could it have been only five or six years ago? – she had said to her mother, "Idealism, politics. I've learned from your experience how ineffectual they are. I'll take a short-cut, forget the grand solutions and do what I can." Which she found to be even less effectual: All she did was patch up people who were fighting for the grand solutions, so they could go back into the firing line. How wise, how practical she had imagined herself to be; how self-satisfied and uncommitted she really had been. The vengeful gods had exacted their price for her arrogance, and Michael had been one of their instruments.

She is forgetting what he looks like, who he really is: the young crusader who has taken on the oppressor out of love for humanity; or the dark, bitter man who has sworn vengeance against the enemy.

Looming ahead is the koppie, a black, rounded mass against a starry, purple-black sky. In daylight she can see the house where she grew up; at night it disappears into dark anonymity. A string of lights outlines the road that runs below its crest, and behind the trees lit-up houses flash out their message: people are living here. Once they had been complacent people, certain of their right to privilege, to dominance. Today they imprison themselves behind iron bars and high fences and sleep with revolvers on their bedside tables. She guesses the location of her parents' home, now her mother's home, by the radio mast, identifiable only as a vertical row of lights, which stands about a hundred metres to the left of the house, on the peak of the koppie. If she had not felt so shakey, she might have driven up the pass to the koppie. Instead, she turns into the road that will take her to Crown Mines.

To keep awake she turns on the radio. With a bit of luck she might pick up the BBC World Service; news on local channels is heavily censored. The crackling fades and she hears a cool Oxonian voice.

'... to restore peace in South Africa's burning townships. Under these sweeping Emergency regulations, security forces will be given almost unlimited powers of arrest and detention. They come into force at midnight. Virtually the whole of the Vaal Triangle and the Eastern Cape will be under emergency rule. It is the first time since the Sharpeville uprising, twenty-five years ago, that the Government has resorted to such drastic measures to quell unrest...'

Sara switches off the radio. Any pretence of respect for law has been abandoned. Between them and the People's Courts, a state of anarchy will now prevail.

She remembers the young boy – he couldn't have been more than twelve – whose back had been pocked with birdshot fired by the police as he ran away from the People's Court in 15th Street. Tear-streaked, he lay on his stomach as she wiped down his back with warm water and disinfectant. "Don't let your friends cut out the pellets," she had told him. "It'll become infected and you'll have to go to hospital. They have not penetrated deeply and will probably push themselves out." "How? Well, the tissue will form a little wall around each pellet and seal them off with fibrin and white cells, and being foreign bodies, they'll probably be rejected. I know, it's difficult to understand, but please take my word for it and don't try to prise them out. Would you like to be a doctor when you grow up? No? I don't blame you."

As she turns into the street where she lives, she sees an unfamiliar car parked near her house. It is too late to turn back; they must have seen her. She drives up to the house and parks her car behind theirs. Two men step out of the car and come towards her.

177

"Are you looking for someone?" she asks.

"Don't you remember us, Miss, uh, Dr Singer? You've become a doctor since we last met," Lieutenant Viljoen says. Sergeant Donges, who is standing at the other door, smirks.

Sara remembers them, only too well. "No," she says, "I have a poor memory for faces."

"Perhaps you'll recognise us in the light. Will you invite us into your house?"

"The last time we met," Sara is too weary to keep up the pretence, "you came into my house uninvited. What's changed?"

Michael had moved in with her a few months before, and his workroom was still in a chaotic state. Three of his favourite posters hung on the walls; everything else lay on the floor in untidy piles. THE TROUBLE WITH GENERAL ELECTIONS, one poster read, IS THAT YOU DON'T KNOW WHICH GENERAL YOU ARE ELECTING. THE NEXT WAR WILL DETERMINE NOT WHAT IS RIGHT BUT WHAT IS LEFT, another warned. The third poster showed the world in flames: IGNORE IT AND IT WILL GO AWAY. He and Zalman had argued heatedly about pollution, the hole in the ozone layer, and the destruction of rain forests. When the socialist millennium comes in, Michael had claimed, all ecological problems will be solved. I heard the same about anti-Semitism, Zalman had retorted. Meantime, the socialist countries are causing even more pollution than the wicked capitalists. You've been reading *Time Magazine* again, Michael replied. They argued interminably, striking sparks off one another, but loved one another unconditionally.

"Nice and tidy," Lieutenant Viljoen says as he and Sergeant Donges follow Sara into the house. "You can see he doesn't live here any more."

She opens the doors to all the rooms, then sits down quickly. Her knees are buckling under her. She wants something to drink but will not put on the kettle until they leave.

"Hell, man," Lt Viljoen says as he looks carefully into all the rooms, "When I first walked into his room and saw all that mess, I thought, how am I ever going to work my way through all that junk? But I managed, and what interesting things I found there in all that rubbish. You must admit it, Dr Singer, he was an untidy young fellow. And very careless."

Their old trick: drawing you in, making an accomplice of you. Sara ignores his easy familiarity, hoping they will go away without a search. She cannot remember if she has destroyed the latest of the unsigned postcards Michael had sent her through Zalman. 'Spy Ring Uncovered in Jewish Aged Home.' She imagines the Director's face as Zalman is taken in for questioning. That's what comes from playing Fah Fee with the blacks, he would intone sanctimoniously. I always knew the old man was up to no good.

"To what do I owe the honour of this visit?" she asks in her crispest voice. "I have had a long day at the Clinic and am not in the mood for amiable conversation right now. In other words, what exactly do you want from me?"

"Direct question gets a direct answer," Viljoen says, sitting down on the couch where she and Michael had sat, aeons ago, trying to make sense of her vegetable co-op list. "Michael is back in the country and we're looking for him. Have you seen him?"

He does not require an answer. Her pallor tells him everything.

Viljoen joins Donges who has remained standing at the front door.

"You haven't heard. Yet. Okay. But if you know what's good for you, you'll contact us when you do. Immediately. If you don't, you'll be in for it. Like being charged with harbouring a terrorist. We know you go around saving the lives of township terrorists, Dr Singer. But don't try to be smart with us. We don't play around, as you know. Happy dreams."

She waits till she hears their car pull away, then sits on the sofa and weeps. When she recovers, she dials her mother's number.

"I'm fine, Ma, don't panic. I'm at home. Just a little tired. Heavy day at the Clinic, as usual. Would you like to come over for a bite? I've got some lasagne in the freezer. Dad's coming? That's a change. Any chance for a reconciliation? No? Well, I didn't really expect it. Good I didn't drop in after work. I hate

179

to see the house dismantled, your lives dismantled. After all, I grew up there. Yes, I know. Farewells aren't easy. Please, I'm a grown woman; you're not deserting me. You know how well I cope. Nothing fazes me. It's your life, for goodness sake. About time you thought about yourself first. And if that's what you feel, don't let Dad or anyone else stop you. I love you too. I'll drop in tomorrow, after work."

Nothing fazes me, she repeats to her misted image in the bathroom mirror. She sits on the edge of the bath, drinking her coffee as the water trickles in. We were too happy, Michael, loved one another too much though we always hesitated to say it. Joked and made light of it. Romeo and Juliet indeed. Superstitious dread, I reckon. I felt it on that hot November afternoon when I rode pillion on your motor cycle. This can't last, I thought. What right had I to be so happy in this terrible world? And I was right, I was right.

TWENTY-ONE

"Sara! Where are you phoning from? Crown Mines? Thank goodness. I'm NOT panicking. It's just that you sound so exhausted, so, distant, and with all that trouble in Alex. Thanks, not tonight. I'm waiting for Dad. Our farewell. It's not going to be easy, after all these years. I feel I'm breaking up, well, if not exactly the happy home, certainly your home, Avi's, Dad's, my own. I know everyone's got their own homes, but the place you grew up in, the place where you raised your children, well, that's different from any other home you'll ever have. It should be there to come back to, a den where you can take refuge. It's harder than I imagined. And I hate leaving you alone, in such times, doing such work. Nothing fazes you? That's fortunate. I'll miss you. More than I can say. And of course I'll come back if things don't work out. But I've got to give it a try. Lay old ghosts, that sort of thing. You'll come tomorrow evening? Good. At the hotel. Yes, the auctioneers move in tomorrow morning. I love you. Goodnight."

It's a strain, hiding her anxiety. Nothing fazes me indeed. Does Sara expect her to believe that, working in the hell Alexandra and the other townships have become? She'd been offered

181

a job in paediatrics at the General Hospital but turned it down; I'm needed here, she told Ruth. She always looks tired, tense. At twenty-seven her skin has lost its glow, there are dark rings under her eyes, and her beautiful blond hair, cut into a bob, is drab yellow. As far as Ruth knows, she does not date anyone, though she occasionally speaks about a doctor called Reggie with whom she works at the Clinic. In an earlier age, she might have gone into a nunnery. Or sailed off to the Crimea. Goodness knows what sights have transformed her mischievous, green eyes into weary, veiled eyes.

Ruth puts another log onto the fire. It is difficult to heat the large, half-empty lounge which no longer looks like home. The only other home Ruth had found difficult to leave had been in Tel Aviv, almost forty years ago.

"Lama barachtem?" Daniel's Israeli family had asked many years later when Ruth and Daniel had returned to visit.

Barachtem: from the verb livroach, to flee, flit, run away; past tense, plural. In this context: why did you desert us, 'us' being the family, the country, the austere conditions which Israelis had imposed upon themselves in order to take in the survivors of the Holocaust, and the Jewish refugees from Iraq, Yemen, Syria and other Arab countries. They should have said "Lama azavtem', why did you leave. It would have been more polite. But they wanted to express disapproval.

"Ven men hot kinder in wiegen, lost'n menschen tzu-frieden," Ruth's grandmother used to say when untested people made judgements on others. When you have children in the cradle ... They could not have known that one day they would follow their own children into the scramble for material wealth, chop down their cherished orange groves and transform them into real estate.

Ruth draws the cardigan around her shoulders. Winter is a season well-suited to her mood. An icy wind is blowing across the ridge; the weather bureau has predicted snow on the 'berg. Only yesterday it had been autumn. Now she too has lost her reds and browns and golds; she feels chilled to the heart.

It had been spring when she and Daniel first visited his cousins on their small-holding, about thirty kilometres from Tel Aviv. A full moon was rising in a purple sky and the fragrance of orange blossoms had been intoxicating. Had they really been so hopeful, so naive? She looks at her watch. Daniel is late as usual. Even on the evening of their farewell.

Lama barachtem: the phrase has haunted her for years. It will be used again when she leaves South Africa, in its English translation and in the singular: Lama baracht? And her friends might with justice ask: Why are you running away? Why are you leaving us in the darkest period of our history? Been kicked in the teeth by your BC friends? No place for whites in Africa? Don't go; things are changing. There is a place for whites in the struggle. Ah, you of little faith, are you tired of carrying the White Madam's burden? You have struggled valiantly under it for so long, in great comfort, persevere a little longer. Had enough of your privileged life? Try living in Soweto. Okay, that's tokenism. You can't write here? Don't grieve. Your former friends said you were irrelevant anyway. But why Israel where you can't even use the tools of your trade. You're tired of words, you want to paint, you need to find out who you are before you die. So's they can engrave the right name on your headstone? The mystic air of Safad indeed. It's probably polluted as Hell, not least from all the fundamentalist rubbish that's breathed into it. Aha, you want to slough off all guilts, to paint yourself into a peaceful corner. If it's peace you're after, don't go to Israel. If you want to opt out of history go to New Zealand or Australia, where the sun's fixed at noon and the shadows cling to your soles like dog crap, a long way from your nose. They 'pacified' their natives, retaining their names for rivers, mountains, suburbs and streets. Whykickamoocow. Kickatinalong. That kind of thing. You won't find peace in Israel. There the shadows are long and dark, and every stone tells a story.

My roots are tugging at me, Ruth will have to explain, risking the banal; who isn't digging for roots these days? With my living bonds attenuated, I am drawn to my ancestors, she will say. Not those I've displaced on this hill; my own ancestors. These days I sing songs my mother taught me, quote my grandmother's sayings, and am haunted by my father's family who remonstrate from their mass grave: why have you, who never knew us, forsaken us?

Ruth looks around the draughty, half-empty room. Tomorrow the auctioneers move in. She is surprised how easy it is to shed possessions. Daniel has taken what he needs for his apartment; Sara wants nothing but her old teddy bear, and Selina has moved the dining-room suite to her house in the homelands. She and Ruth embraced and wept when they said goodbye. They have not seen Luke for months and rarely mention his name, but the pain is there.

Sara has invited her to stay in Crown Mines till she leaves for Israel, but Ruth is going to a hotel. She needs neutral surroundings in which to sever ties. She has said goodbye to most of her family and friends. There remains only the *Skelm* connection. She will phone Nicholas, who is teaching metaphysical poetry at the University of Cape Town. He is writing poetry again. It will be a short call; they have little to say to one another. Later she will have coffee with David and tease him a little about not migrating to Lettland as he once threatened. He has told her that aspiring black poets still bring their work to him. Mogorosi, Simon and Vusi are not on her list, but she would have liked to see Thami, the Soweto Renaissance man, once again. And Mandla Magwaza, the People's Poet, and all the other young poets with such faith in the Word.

After that fateful meeting in the Laager, she had helped Nicholas wind down Skelm Publications. Other publishers have since jumped onto the black writing bandwagon and are turning it into a profitable business: Black writing, sanitised, has become fashionable. It even features on the curricula of some universities.

Vusi and Thami left *Skelm* almost immediately, and moved into a suite of offices which houses not only the new black writers' organisation, but also a publishing house. Vusi is full-time secretary of the black writers' society, and Thami is editor of its broadsheet. Readers have been promised a journal to replace the defunct *Skelm,* but so far nothing has appeared. Mogorosi, the chief editor of the black publishing house, now sits behind an enormous desk in a three-piece suit, selecting only the best from the pile of manuscripts in front of him. He has acquired standards.

Where are they getting money from, Nicholas had wondered when they swung into action immediately after the dissolution of the non-racial writers' organisation. He soon found out. A polite letter from Skelm Publications' overseas funders informed him that it had always been their intention to fund a black publishing house. After Mr Simon Sibandla's recent visit, they had realised that *Skelm* was a white-run organisation. While they appreciated Nicholas' efforts, they were sure he would understand why they were diverting their funds to Mr Sibandla and his organisation.

Nicholas had been stunned by Simon's duplicity, hurt by Mogorosi's betrayal. "They knew I wanted to hand over," he had said. "Why didn't they discuss it with me?" "Don't patronise us, white man," Simon might have answered. "We decide when and how we take over." Ruth often wonders whether Simon ever discovered the true identity of Nocha Nakasa. Jenny had walked out at the same time as Vusi and Thami, but did not get a job in the new publishing organisation. "They haven't enough money for another salary," she told Nicholas, "so meantime I'm working as an insurance clerk. Soul-destroying work." "It's not because you're white?" Nicholas had responded with uncharacteristic bitterness. "No," she replied. "I'm regarded as a white African. There's simply no money." "They should take a cut in their salaries and create one for you, as we did for Vusi," he had said.

Ruth wonders whether the old *Skelm* group still holds poetry readings in the townships, and whether Mandla Magwaza strides the boards of local churches and community halls, declaiming his epic poem: "Africa my beginning, and Africa my ending..." She has no way of knowing. She has not been to the black townships since the recent wave of violence.

She has heard, however, that the trade union movement had spawned a new people's poet who exhorts his audiences to rise up against the racist capitalist pigs and show them where the real power lies. No trace of Eliot in his oratory.

Why is Daniel so late? His excuse used to be a board meeting or a working dinner with his salesmen. He has changed so much since he was forced to sell out his share in the furniture factory and relinquish his job as managing director. He had always had a good, if paternalistic, relationship with the black workers. Too good, his Board of Directors had complained. "Crack the whip, increase productivity," they demanded. "Profits are falling and the shareholders are not pleased." Matters worsened when the wave of consumer boycotts throughout the country had affected retail outlets.

Soon after he was retired, the factory had been hit by a massive strike. "Let them handle the trade unions," Daniel had said bitterly. "I'm pleased I'm not there, though I do miss being in the mainstream." "The mainstream of what?" Ruth had asked. "You've always been an avid reader, you love music, and you used to enjoy painting." "You're right," Daniel said. "Now I'll do all the things I've never had time for." He moved his computer into Avi's bedroom, put up book shelves, fished out his easel from the garage, then paced the floor above Ruth's study, wondering what it was he had always wanted to do. He raided the fridge, put on weight, played golf twice a week, and every domestic bicker ignited a conflict at a deeper level, piercing the scab of old wounds. There were times when he seemed a total stranger.

She remembered the evening, many years ago, when she, Daniel, Lola and Paul had talked about differing attitudes to money. "Don't be so snotty about it," Lola had leapt to Daniel's defence. "You're a beneficiary of his business success." That was the first time Ruth had become aware of their special relationship. Not too late for them to get together again, Ruth thinks, if Lola would take time off from her Rosa Luxembourg act. These days she is speaking from every public platform in town.

It was after they had broken with the Sterns that she and Daniel had withdrawn even further from one another. He went abroad often, stayed late at the office, came home with whisky on his breath and lipstick on his shirt. She had retreated into her writing. But when he forbade Luke to come to the house – he's a jailbird, he said, and in these uncertain, violent times, I don't want tsotsis on my premises – she realised how irreconcilable their differences were. "After all these years," had been his bitter incredulous refrain when she suggested they separate. "We're not getting younger, we need one another, we've been through so much together…"

The door bell startles Ruth. Daniel must find it strange to ring the bell of the place he called home for twenty years. Ruth takes a deep breath. She will remain calm and patient, but will not allow him to stir up guilts.

"Hello, Daniel," she says.

"Hello, Ruth." He looks slim and attractive in his new tweed suit. His hair, altogether white, has been stylishly cut and makes him look younger. There's a new woman in his life. She feels a twinge of regret and remembers the good years.

"Have you eaten?" she asks out of habit.

"Of course. You didn't exactly invite me to dinner."

"In this mess?" Her arms describe a wide circle, taking in the curtainless windows, the half-empty lounge, the packed boxes in the corner. "Sit at the fire. I've got coffee on the boil."

She is pleased he is looking well, that there is a new woman in his life: the suit, the weight loss, attest to that. She wants him to remake his life so that she can get on with hers, free of guilt, of regret. And yet … As she pours the coffee, she remembers how hard it had been to put the past behind her. If she weakens now, she's lost. She takes the coffee into the lounge.

"You're looking well," they say at the same time. They laugh, breaking the tension.

"New man in your life?" he asks casually, taking the coffee from her. She shakes her head.

"Old man?" he persists. Her regret dissolves. The familiar panic wells up; he is slipping into his interrogatory mode. "Like

Paul, for example? He's back in Johannesburg, I believe, and has been living the life of what, in more innocent times, used to be described as that of a gay bachelor. I've been wondering whether your determination to separate has anything to do with the Sterns' break-up."

"Nothing at all. The after-shock of our emotional muddle must have hit us at the same time. I haven't seen Paul in fifteen, twenty years, I forget how long. Nor am I likely to at this stage. Remember, I leave for Israel in a few days' time."

"But you'd like to see him."

Ruth stands up. "Daniel, this is the last time we'll be together for a long time. Let's separate on a civilised note. I'm glad you're looking well. I might have asked if there's a new woman in your life, but I didn't."

"You are now. No one special," he mumbles. He looks around the room. "You've certainly disposed of the past, packed it up neatly, labelled it, and now it's ready for the refuse heap. Past for sale, outlived reason for existence. It feels so strange, so spooky, it could be happening in one of your stories, not in real life. Except that you wrote it, or rather, wrote it off."

"It's surprisingly easy to divest oneself of possessions." She steers the conversation away from dangerous ground.

He looks at her and for the first time in years, she feels he is seeing her. The look is sharp, observant, ironic, and seems to peer into her very depths: he once knew her so well.

"You don't change, do you?" he says. "None of us does, I suppose. Still kidding yourself you live on fresh air and clean money. Easy to divest oneself of possessions indeed. Isn't money possessions? What about the income you're going to live on from your investment in Escom, bought with the proceeds of possessions like this house, the car, shares, the furniture?"

If I cry now I'm lost. Ruth takes a deep breath and smiles, somewhat tremulously.

"Touché, as an old friend of yours might have said. But you're right, Daniel. We don't change, and my particular form of hypocrisy is no more attractive than yours."

"I still feel we could've made a go of it. Where will you live?"

188

"I'll find a room in Safad."

"A room, in Safad? With a landlady measuring how much hot water you use? After having lived in this house? You're full of romantic notions."

"'...And makes one little room, an everywhere,'" she quotes, leaving out the preceding line, 'For love, all love of other sights controls...' There has been no mention of love between them for years.

"Whenever you're on the defensive, you quote poetry," he says petulantly.

He finishes his coffee and puts the cup down on a cardboard box. For a while they sit in silence. She should put another log on the fire, but she does not wish to prolong the farewell.

"Well," he says, standing up. "I guess that's it. No sense in prolonging goodbyes. I can't believe it's happening. I just want you to know that if you need anything, any help, you know ... It won't be easy on your own. And don't worry about Sara. I'll keep an eye on her. We've been getting on well lately."

She gets up quickly and embraces him. The familiar smell of his skin which she has loved at times, hated at times, seeps through his aftershave lotion. They had lived in the same street, started school on the same day, been in the Movement together, gone to Israel, had children ... All she need say is, let's try again. We'll let one another live, and perhaps it'll work out, this time.

"Goodbye, Daniel," she weeps onto the lapel of his new suit which smells of tailor's shop, like her father's workshop, where she had been witness to other betrayals, to other heartbreak. "Be well. You'll always be my friend and I'll be yours."

He kisses her on the forehead, holds her close, then lets himself out of the house. A last look, a few regrets, some relief, no mention of love. What has it all been about? Meaningless. Everything is meaningless. She understands nothing. And if existence is indeed meaningless, she will have to face the void. She has been shored against despair by fiction, by her writing, and by asking unanswerable questions. But now she has been stripped of her last defence: she has lost her voice, can write no longer. Somewhere she read that to write a poem after Auschwitz

189

is barbarous. And to write about Auschwitz is unthinkable. Had her art been stronger, her life might have been more meaningful. But perhaps there is life after love, after art. Perhaps she is only suffering from fictional fatigue. She is weary of the heavy burden of bearing witness, to her forebears' tragedy, to this country's tragedy. Let photographers record the turbulence of the century. She will look into the heart of a flower and try to reproduce its essence. And it could take the rest of her life to do so.

Ruth puts on her cardigan and goes outside. She shivers. The pressure of mortality seems to push through the dark trees at the end of the garden; there is so little time left. She looks into the dark valley on the far side of the golf course where the river, stagnant and stinking, lies trapped in shallow pools. Then up towards the Aged Home where centuries ago her mother lay dying beneath starched sheets. She must go to the cemetery, take leave of the dead. Beyond the Homes and houses is the dry winter veld, on which necklaces of fire are burning, in ever-widening circles. The air is icy, acrid with the smell of burning grass and who knows what else? Somewhere, beyond the white suburbs, lies Alexandra township, imprisoned beneath a pall of smoke.

"You can have the house back!" she calls to the Ancestors of the bush people who are hovering over the primeval rocks, watching, waiting. "Move in! Dance on our ruins! We should never have displaced you."

The radio mast blinks silently into the night, contemptuous of the history which lies buried beneath it.

TWENTY-TWO

Difficult to write. Strength comes and goes. Lola will be here soon. If I'm writing she'll think I'm better, no matter that I gasp for breath, tethered to the oxygen like dog on leash.

Not her day for visiting but I sent the usual message: uncle needs another book. Code for, received another postcard from Michael. Oif di eltere yahren, in my dotage, I have joined the underground. Under the ground is where I should be already. Lola insists we speak in riddles. Says her phone is tapped. Why not? Dead cats at front door, fire bombs in lounge, tyres slashed. Hit squads think she's dangerous! Her connection with that black woman necklaced a few weeks ago. But Lola's no Rosa. Shocked by the brutality – those blood-red nails, she kept saying – and her failure in judgement. Never suspected the woman was a police spy. No longer mentions it. Knows how to cut. Wish I had her gift.

Dropped off to sleep. Get tired so easily. Feel stronger now.

When Lola hears 'another book', she drops everything and comes; she lives for Michael's cards. He must have bought all the Royal Family greeting cards in England: Di with her

children, Di in the slums, Di with her mother-in-law; Prince
Charles frowning, Prince Charles smiling, Prince Charles with
hands in pockets. Princess Anne on a horse ... Wicked boy. Spot
the horse, he wrote. The cards are posted from London and
arrive weeks, sometimes months, after date of writing. Well-
travelled cards, with only a line or two to say he's well. Strange
he's such a fan of the royals, Lola has commented, perplexed.

Sara enjoys the postcards; she's pleased Michael has not lost
his sense of the absurd. Remarkable young woman. She's
thrown herself into the heart of the struggle, though she suspects there may not be a solution. Lola, for all her radicalisation, remains a social worker: identify problem, apply social
therapy, solution follows. No sense of the tragic.

I no longer address Lola. A sign this isn't meant for her. I'll
stop writing and ask Mr Sibiya to burn all the notebooks
together with the photographs in the suitcase. Some heirloom.
The self-ennobling ravings of a superfluous old man. In a dying
language, noch. But such an auto da fé could cause trouble for
Mr Sibiya. Must devise another plan.

I write one or two sentences at a time. These few lines have
taken me almost an hour. Still no Lola.

I also asked the Sister to contact Sara at the Clinic and say
Uncle Zalman is missing her. She knows what that means –
even if she doesn't realise I actually miss her! I hope she doesn't
bump into Lola. Tangled emotions from Lola's youth. Jealous
of Sara's mother. If she's like Sara, I understand. She's gone to
Israel. Sara misses her. Lola misses out.

Shocked by Michael's latest card. No royal family this time.
An aerial view of Johannesburg with Brixton Tower in the
foreground. Michael hates the Tower as much as the radio mast
on the ridge. Symbols, he says. Postmarked Johannesburg, three
days ago.

They had to put me back on oxygen. Not that I value life,
but I want to see Michael one more time. In my dreams I
confuse him with Leibala. Now that he's near, they can give me
any therapy they like: pummel my legs, thump my back, knead
my stomach – anything. You'll live, the physiotherapist said to

me this morning; you're a tough old bird. Pickled in vitriol, I told her.

Something has delayed Lola. I expected her two hours ago.

All this moaning and groaning around me. Six of us in this ward. I am the healthiest. Thank goodness I can still read. Otherwise I would die of boredom and depression.

Since I've been ill, Mr Sibiya visits me every day, always with a broom or yellow duster. When anyone walks into the ward, he begins sweeping or polishing. Mr Sibiya, I say, why should you not visit your old friend? They will say I am lazy, he replies. After thirty-six years, Mr Sibiya? He shrugs. He keeps me in touch with the outside world. He tells me which numbers have been pulled by the China, who has won, who has lost. I have lost my taste for Fah Fee, but I do not tell him this. I humour him by inventing innocuous dreams and he humours me by selecting the numbers. Why bother him with my nightmares? He has his own. He is much changed since his accident a few weeks ago. All I know is that he was concussed in an explosion in the township and spent a week in hospital. He never talks about his family. I suspect a tragedy.

Lola has arrived. She greets the other patients hurriedly, appears agitated...

"How are you, Zalman?" Lola sits down on a chair next to his bed. With deliberate movements, he puts his notebook on the bedside table. She does not seem to notice.

"I am better. I want to go back to my own room." If he does not grumble, she will think he is really sick.

"Don't rush it. I spoke to the doctor. He says pneumonia in the elderly..."

"Old, Lola, old. Don't be diplomatic. Elderly. At eighty-six I'm entitled to be old. Old enough to die. But I'm in no hurry to oblige anyone."

He leans over, opens the drawer and takes out Michael's postcard. If she faints, she faints. This is a hospital, after all. She takes the postcard and presses it to her chest without looking at it. She is very distracted.

"Something terrible happened this morning, Zalman. That's why I'm late. There was an explosion at our offices early this morning. Thank God no one was hurt. The watchman heard noises, went outside to investigate, and escaped injury. They placed explosives in the lift shaft. All six floors are damaged. Can't say how badly. I always feared … Too vulnerable … The fire brigade is there right now, assessing the damage. All those records. All that work. The building's been cordoned off. Too dangerous to enter. Some of us went there. The vestibule's caved in, the tapestry must be in shreds. I've told you about the tapestry. Made of felt, with Peace embroidered in six languages. Peace is shattered. And that sad-eyed Christ figure. At least he lived long enough to see the pass book scrapped, if not influx control. All this bombing and killing. Will it never end?"

"Lola, you're making me dizzy. So much information. My little brain can't take it in."

"Sorry, I got carried away." She takes her glasses out of her handbag and looks at the postcard.

"Johannesburg," she whispers. "Johannesburg. Zalman! What's going to happen?"

"I'll tell you what's going to happen. The Sister's going to come into the ward and ask you to leave because you're upsetting the patients. Nothing's going to happen. He will lie low. Only don't expect to see him…"

"Of course not." Lola straightens up. "But he may come here. As he did before he left. The Home is safe. Or he may go to her…"

"He won't endanger anyone. He knows she's being watched, you're being watched. He'd only come here if he was desperate. He's not a hot-head."

Zalman wishes he believed it. Lately guerilla activity has been stepped up. Military and police targets have been attacked, but civilians have also been injured. Only yesterday he read that an arms cache had been found on a farm in the Western Transvaal. It contained AK 47 rifles, ammunition, hand grenades and plastic explosives. Notes and sketches had also been found. The police had been led to it by a captured, no doubt tortured, 'terrorist'. He is sure Lola reads the newspapers very carefully.

"You're right," she sighs. "His function no doubt is political. He's so good with sketches, cartoons, posters. No violence, not him ... I must go back to the offices, to see if they've been able to enter the building. They brought a crane. Thought they could get in through the first floor windows. The vestibule's completely ... And that tapestry ... I'll leave the card here," she says, putting it into the drawer. "Better not have it on me. I'm pleased to see you're feeling better. I'll see you on Friday."

"Goodbye, Bailka," he says.

"Zalman! I'm Lola. You're confused..."

"Yes, yes. I sometimes get mixed up. For a moment I thought you were my sister."

Zalman adjusts his oxygen mask and lies back. Lola's visit, short as it was, has exhausted him. So has his writing. No more of that. Lola never really cared about his memoirs, and Michael does not have access to them. One generation and a rich language has become a secret code. The dead are claiming their own.

As he dozes off, he sees the avenue of trees which leads into the park. Always those trees. It is dusk and the Sabbath strollers have returned to their homes. The last light fades from the sky and the canopy of ancient trees presses down on him, blocking off all air. He walks faster, breathing heavily, making for the open space in the centre of the park, where, in summer, the young ones lie on the sweet green grass, talking and laughing, calling out the names of their friends as they pass, never dreaming they are lying on their grave. He hears the wind in the trees, but no air reaches him. As he hurries towards the gate, his breath coming in uneven gasps, he hears thundering horse hoofs, coming nearer, growing louder. Then the dark rider bursts out of the wood, shouting, "Run, run! Save yourselves! The beasts are coming!"

"You're all right, Zalman. You must have fallen asleep and the oxygen mask slipped off. It's all right, it's all right!"

Gasping for breath he sits up. Sara is standing next to him, holding his hand.

"It was so dark, in the park. Where they dug the mass grave, afterwards. Ravings of an old man, Sara. Holding on to life for a while longer. When the dream ends, I'll join them, but I never let it end. Is it evening already?" He tries to get up.

"No. I'm on night duty so I came this afternoon. Don't talk now. I'm not going away."

"The postcard." He motions towards the drawer in the bedside table. "No queen, no princess. Only the Tower ... He's here."

"I know." Sara says quietly. "They told me. Weeks ago. I haven't seen him."

Zalman dozes off. When he wakes, Sara is still sitting next to him, leaning back in the chair, her eyes shut.

"You are tired," he says.

"Yes. There's been a lot of work at the Clinic."

"You must see terrible things, in the township."

She nods.

"How can you bear it?"

"I don't know. It's the people, I suppose. I draw strength from them. They bend before the horror and endure their anguish with unbelievable stoicism. When they resurface, they are stronger, able to sing and dance, not only in defiance, also with joy. Joy at being alive, in that hell. And without bitterness, Zalman. With tremendous hope. I don't know where they dredge it up from. It's as though they understand their real power, and hold on to it, through all that oppression. I coast along on that, I reckon. As for the violence, the brutalisation..." She shudders. "If they can endure it, so can I."

"You don't have to endure it," Zalman says. "You can leave. Join your mother in Israel, go elsewhere, anywhere."

Sara shakes her head. "I can't leave. Not before I meet Michael again."

"What will happen, with you and Michael?"

"It's been a long time. We were already having serious differences before he left. He had talked about the armed struggle, meeting violence with violence. And that was before his detention. Nothing is solved with violence, I used to say. I don't know any longer. He was also certain that something better, more just and equitable would follow on this horror, but I'm not sure about that either. Never was. I have this dream where I'm searching for him in a crowd and can't find him. Then someone comes up and says, I'm Michael, but it's a stranger ... Zalman, I'm afraid we've lost one another..."

He pats her hand awkwardly. "I'm a stupid old man for asking. I just want for you both to be happy. But tell me. What about your life? Do you go out, see friends, go to bioscope to see a movie sometimes? Or are you always stitching up people?"

She laughs. "Of course I go out. And I've made very good friends with my co-workers at the Clinic. We've been through a lot together. Life may be grim, Zalman, but the world is beautiful, and I enjoy being alive in it. I may move out of Crown Mines though. I don't feel at ease there any more, especially after the burglary and that mess they made in the bath. Besides, most of my neighbours have gone into hiding, whether they need to or not. I hardly recognise them these days: dyed, coiffeured hair, elegant clothes, make-up. You remember the old uniform: jeans and T-shirts. If I don't recognise them, the Special Branch won't either. I suspect they're enjoying their disguises."

She leans over and kisses him on the forehead.

"I have to leave, Zalman. See you soon. And phone whenever you want to. Who knows, you may even get a special visitor one of these days."

"I am expecting only the Angel of Death."

"Don't be morbid. You'll outlive us all."

"God forbid."

He watches her walk towards the door, tall, slim, her hair like a golden halo around her head. As she reaches the door, Mr Sibiya comes in. They stop and look at one another, as though in recognition. Mr Sibiya lowers his head, and, duster in hand, comes towards Zalman's bed. Sara looks back, puzzled, then walks slowly of the ward.

TWENTY-THREE

Zalman never saw the brilliant flash which lit up the dark, moonless sky. Nor did he hear the explosion that echoed through the valley which separates the houses from the Homes. The explosives, the morning newspaper speculated, might have been placed around the radio mast in such a way that it would crash onto the unbuilt section of the ridge. A few sparks, however, had ignited the thatched roof of the house below the mast. It burned down to the ground. Fortunately it was empty; the previous owners had left a few weeks before, and the new tenants had not yet moved in. The arsonists, the newspaper concluded, could not have predicted the direction in which the mast would fall, demonstrating, once again, that it was impossible to separate civilian from government or military targets.

Soon after Sara left, Zalman's breathing had become irregular again, and Mr Sibiya, standing at the foot of his bed, yellow duster in hand, had pressed the emergency bell.

Zalman is now in the Intensive Care Unit. He tosses about restlessly in his narrow cot, dreaming of the dark rider. "Listen to him!" he wants to cry out, but his mouth is stuffed with ash.

History will not be reversed. For the price of a few sea fares they might have been saved. But Leibala would never have left: he had faith in the new society. "Agitator, communist," the townsmen call the dark rider. "Leave our homes and possessions and flee into the wilderness?" "The Nazis are thirty kilometres away," Leibala cries. "Flee for your lives!" "Get out! You always created panic. We know the Germans..." "Let me take my family," he pleads, but the townsmen hold them hostage. He weeps as he embraces his mother, his sister and two brothers, then mounts his horse and rides away. His fate awaits him in Stalingrad.

Zalman sighs and turns onto his side. He has dreamed his nightmare to its end.

Mr Sibiya polishes the door handle till it shines. Only when the night staff come on duty and draw the curtains around Zalman's bed, does he fold up his yellow duster and walk slowly down the corridor.

As he reaches the front door, a burst of fire lights up the houses embedded on the koppie, followed by an explosion that rattles the windows of the Home. Transfixed, Mr Sibiya watches a roof catch fire, its flames singeing the sky. Such a bonfire will be seen through the dust and smoke that hangs over Alexandra Township, and all the people will stand on their rutted roads, looking towards the koppies in the white suburbs. Even the Casspirs will stop dead in their tracks, their guns silent for once. And everyone will understand the message from the ridge.

St Suniti and the Dragon
Suniti Namjoshi

St Suniti and the Dragon is an extended fable. The central theme, of how to live decently and honourably in a cruel and irrational world, is explored through related themes such as sainthood, love, and the anticipation of death. The treatment of this thematic texture is both ironic and fantastic, the imagery ranging from talking flowers to instructive angels, from literary monsters such as Grendel's Dam, to religious icons such as St Sebastian, from the sentient creatures of Indian fable to the western archetype of the life-destroying dragon.

This interplay of themes and images is matched by an interplay of forms, including song, dialogue, narrative, dramatic monologue and lyric, as well as more everyday forms such as postcards and prayers, and diary entries written during the Gulf War. The resulting sequence is at once elegant and elegiac, fearful and funny. It is, in fact, a thoroughly modern fable.

'*St Suniti and the Dragon* illuminates a complex moral investigation of fear (of otherness) and the will to "sainthood". On the surface individualistic and self-investigative, it resonates on allegorical levels with larger issues the women's movement and our society generally are now facing. A wry, sly and very wise variation on the quest.'   – Daphne Marlatt

'I can think of plenty of adjectives to describe *St Suniti and the Dragon*, but not a noun to go with them. It's hilarious, witty, elegantly written, hugely inventive, fantastic, energetic, up to the minute, analytic, touching ... and so on ... With work as original as this, it's easier to fling words at it than to say what it is or what it does.'   – U. A. Fanthorpe

'With harsh lucidity and elegant irony, Namjoshi uses the paradigms of fable to instruct – and reconstruct – our social perceptions.'   – M. Travis Lane

Feminist Fables

(new edition)

Suniti Namjoshi

'There was once a man who thought he could do anything, even be a woman. So he acquired a baby, changed its diapers and fed the damn thing three times a night. He did all the housework, was deferential to men, and got worn out. But he had a brother, Jack Cleverfellow, who hired a wife, and got it all done.'

– The Tale of Two Brothers

Feminist Fables represents an ingenious reworking of fairytales, Greek and Sanskrit mythology, mixed with the author's original material and vivid imagination.

This book is an indispensable feminist classic.

Suniti Namjoshi was born in Bombay, India. She taught for some years at the University of Toronto, and now lives in England. Her books include *The Conversations of Cow*, *The Blue Donkey Fables* and *The Mothers of Maya Diip*.

The Iron Mouth
Beryl Fletcher

1993 Top Twenty Title,
Listener Women's Book Festival, New Zealand

The Iron Mouth follows the narrator, a film-maker, through the process of writing a script. As the script progresses the narrator's life begins to take on elements of the unreal world of scriptwriting. With a central motif of the book and the film being the story of Helen of Troy and the Trojan war, the lives of the characters (in the novel and the film script) take on new meanings.

The novel is set in Auckland, New Zealand and attempts to deconstruct the notion that warfare between male heroes provides the only genuine topic of epic literature. The film maker, Khryse, finds herself unable to separate the structure and form of epic literature from the notions of glory and the narrative excitement of battle.

Beryl Fletcher was born in Auckland in 1938. She has had stories published in anthologies and her work has received international recognition. Her first book, *The Word Burners*, won the 1992 Commonwealth Writers Prize, Best First Book Award for the South-East Asian and Pacific Region, and was selected as a 1991 Top Twenty Title for the Listener Women's Book Festival, New Zealand.